The Ugliness

Part One in
The Ugliness Trilogy

John U. Gunter

ISBN: 0692918043
ISBN-13: 978-0692918043 (JoGun Publishers)

DEDICATION

To Donald Mark Gunter ~
My father, my biggest fan.

1

Arms around her husband's neck, Chloe Apple bounced up and down with excitement. Peter Apple couldn't stop smiling as the two of them exited the doctor's office with the news they'd wanted to hear: They were having another baby. It was great news! They had prayed for a baby boy and now, after three years of trying, they felt that their prayers had been answered. Even so, the couple had chosen not to know the gender until the child was born.

Four-year-old Mila, the soon-to-be big sister, clapped her hands and screamed with joy when she heard the news of the anticipated arrival. All she cared was that she would soon have a live-in play pal, and she could hardly wait.

Peter Apple spent his days working long hours in an automotive factory putting cars and trucks together on an assembly line. He was paid enough to cover rent, put food on the table and enjoy a few luxuries even when Chloe needed to take a lengthy break from her job at the bakery, due to the pregnancy.

Spirits were high and continued to rise as the due date drew near. Peter would sometimes whisper to

Chloe that it didn't make a difference what gender the baby was. He assured her that either way, he was just happy that they were having another child—though he kept his fingers crossed when saying so, and when he prayed, he prayed for a boy! He wanted to be supportive and in truth, he knew he wouldn't love another little girl any less.

Chloe wanted a boy also. She already had her girl, and she loved Mila with all of her being, but they had tried so hard and long for this pregnancy. She thought a little boy would be the perfect addition to their small family. Plus, she knew—even when Peter did his best at trying to convince her that gender wouldn't matter—*she knew* he wanted a little boy to do boy things with. She wanted so badly to give him what he wanted. But she also knew that the child's gender would be in God's hands, not their own.

In the mornings following the discovery of her fertilized tummy, Chloe began getting sick. She would wake from peaceful sleep and have to make a bee-line for the bathroom, retching out the contents of her stomach from the night before. Horrible dreams started, and only became worse as the fetus grew. Memories of one recurring dream plagued her throughout the day. In it, she was going through labor and when she gave birth, the doctor announced the child was a boy. She was happy until he handed her the newborn. The baby had large black eyes, and it spoke to her in a demonic voice. She could never remember what the child said, but it scared her to the core. She would wake from the dream sick and sobbing, with an embedded suspicion that she was carrying something evil.

She told Peter of her hellish nightmares. She said, "Peter, I'm scared. I think there may be something wrong with the baby."

He asked, "What's wrong, sugar? What would make you think that?"

Chloe shuddered inside. She said, "It's these dreams. They keep getting worse. I think the baby might be demonic."

Peter pulled her close and tucked her head into his chest. He said, "It's just stress, babe. You'll see in another month or so. Our baby's going to be perfect."

She wrapped her arms around the man who loved her so deeply. She said, "Oh, I hope so, honey. I really want the baby to be okay."

Peter said, "The dreams are like watching a scary movie, babe. They seem real, but they're not. They're just dreams."

Chloe pulled away and slapped his arm. She said, "Humph. I'm not a child, Peter Clyde Apple."

Peter laughed and put his hands up. He said, "Okay-okay! Such violence, woman."

She laughed and leaned back into his chest. She asked, "Couldn't we at least find out if it's going to be a boy or a girl?"

"No, sugar plum. Let's wait like we've been planning."

"Okay. If that's what you want."

As the fetus grew it began to move throughout most of the day. Mila loved to sit next to her mother and feel the growing child squirm. She didn't care if it was a boy or girl, but she would choose a girl, if she could. She began to daydream about having a little sister to play with, thinking it would be like having a living doll, dressing her and doing her hair; they could have tea parties and bake things. Of course she thought a boy would be fun, too. When it came right down to it, there was no way that her sibling's gender would disappoint her. She already loved the baby.

Mila put her hand on her mother's stomach. She said, "Mommy. If the baby's a boy he's going to play sports, I bet. Maybe even if it's a girl."

"Why do you say that, sweetie?"

"Because it already has so much energy. Don't you think so?"

Chloe kissed Mila's forehead. She said, "Maybe so, sweetie. Time for bed."

The fetus would kick, twist and do what Chloe described as double backflips, keeping her up throughout the night. It seemed to hate when she wasn't moving. Sometimes she would have to get up in the middle of the night, or early morning hours, and pace the floor until the seemingly tireless tummy-dweller decided to stop spinning, kicking, and causing internal havoc. Chloe could rarely relax or sit still without experiencing *Kung-Fu* from within. Her fears of an evil child festered and grew along with the fetus. The thoughts and feelings became stronger after every bad dream, sleepless night, and restless day.

Chloe went through several false labor scares, so when the day came that her water broke, everyone knew the hospital routine—even Mila.

They all buckled in the car. Mila asked, "Is the baby really coming this time, Mommy?"

Chloe panted and clenched her teeth. She said, "*Yesss*, Mila."

Peter said, "Baby girl, let your momma be."

The labor didn't go smoothly. After several hours of intense labor, the doctor made an eerie announcement. He looked up from Chloe's womb, into Peter's eyes, with concern.

He said, "Mr. Apple. Try to keep calm. I'll need to perform a caesarean. Chloe's suffering heavy blood loss now, and the child is breech."

Without waiting for a response from Peter, the doctor turned to the nurse beside him. He said, "Footling breech, prepare general anesthesia and prep for midline longitudinal incision with anabolic prophylaxis, she's hemorrhaging and I'm using mechanical cervical dilation to prevent hypovolemic shock. Let's save Mrs. Apple."

Peter squeezed Chloe's hand and could feel her life force diminishing. He prayed God wouldn't call her home, and he prayed for his unborn child. They had him exit the room as they rushed Chloe away to surgery. Peter paced the waiting room with his friends and family and paused only when saying another prayer. He couldn't imagine his life without Chloe. She meant more to him than he did to himself. There wasn't anything he could do now but talk to God, and that's what he did: He prayed like he'd never prayed before.

Time seemed to stand still, every second an eternity. Everyone waited for news from the doctor with growing anxiety. Those agonizing seconds and minutes turned into hours.

2

Dr. Collins emerged from between the double doors leading to surgery. Walking directly to Peter, with a blank and exhausted expression, he said, "Mrs. Apple survived. The infant is alive and in perfect health."

Peter didn't realize he had been holding his breath until the doctor completed the sentences. He felt an enormous release of pressure, relieved to hear the news. Reflexively, he hugged the doctor. The man stood as stiff as plywood.

Dr. Collins continued. He said, "There were complications and we had to perform an emergency hysterectomy to save the life of your wife." Peter released him. The doctor continued, "She won't be able to bear any more children. Also, every patient is different and so is recovery time. The length of her stay with us depends on her pain tolerance and inflammation levels. When she does leave she will need to avoid strenuous work. I wouldn't recommend her doing any heavy lifting—nothing over 10 pounds, and no running, walking upstairs, or other types of athletics for fourteen to sixteen weeks."

Peter said, "No problem, Doc, just patch her up and

get her home—she'll be taken care of."

"Yes, well, we'll do our best to promote a speedy recovery. She won't be able to have visitors for several hours. If you'd like to see the infant, go to the newborn observatory down the hall and on the left."

"Thank you doctor. I'll pay my bill, but I don't think I'll ever be able to repay *you*."

Dr. Collins looked Peter in the eye. He said, "Take care of your wife and your newborn son, Mr. Apple. No one can ask more of you than that."

The doctor turned and made his exit before his words sank in. A smile spread across Peter's face. He had a newborn *son*. His prayers had been answered in so many ways—Peter was overwhelmed with gratitude. Tears threatened in the corners of his eyes when he heard Mila's voice soft and meek. She asked, "What did the doctor say, Daddy?"

Peter knelt down and hugged her. He said, "Your momma's going to be okay, sweetheart. Let's go see your baby brother."

Mila beamed. She asked, "I have a brother?"

"That's right, munchkin."

Her face turned downcast. She asked, "What about mommy, Daddy? Is mommy hurt badly?"

Peter gave her a kiss on the cheek. He said, "She's going to be just fine, baby girl."

Standing, he took Mila's hand, then turned towards the small crowd a few feet away and announced Chloe's condition—then waved for them to follow. He said, "Let's all go say hello to my boy!"

Peter held Mila up so she could see her little brother, as family and friends snapped pictures for their albums. Seeing the baby through the glass wasn't enough for Peter. He summoned a nurse and asked when it would be possible to hold his son.

The nurse said, "It won't be long, sir. You have a lively one. He has the most powerful set of lungs! I dare say he could be superhuman." She laughed, a hen like sound. "I'll come get you as soon as he's cleared for contact."

Less than an hour passed watching the nurses fussing over the baby, taking him in and out of the observation room, performing tests. Then they told Peter he could hold his son. Peter went into the observatory and watched as the nurse gathered up the tiny little breathing bundle. He looked into the infant's eyes and felt a swell of pride. When the nurse handed the baby to Peter, he brought him to the window for everyone to get a closer look at the little one whom they'd all come to see.

There was no expression that could be uttered to convey the joy he felt holding his infant boy, knowing Chloe would be at his side again soon.

3

Chloe was home and having minor complications from her surgery. She could move around on her own, but she had difficulties taking care of Barry. They named the new addition after Peter's grandfather. Barry Pete Apple was his full name, and he didn't care to let his parents get much sleep. They were learning what the nurse meant about Barry's super lungs. It had been six weeks since his birth, and Peter had tended to Barry's every need for the first four, but he'd had to return to work, so the responsibility of the infant's needs now fell upon Chloe. Her only relief was when Peter returned from work.

Usually the diaper-changing fell singularly at Chloe's feet. Peter was the first to discover Barry's peculiar habit of waiting until his diaper was off to urinate or even defecate. Peter had been sprayed with enough urine and feces splatter that he refused to change any more of Barry's diapers at one point. What really rubbed the disturbed dad wrong was that Barry would smile, coo, or even let an infant laugh spill over as if he knew exactly what he was doing.

Chloe wasn't going for the no-more-diaper-duty

stance that Peter believed he was going to take. So in compromise, Peter had the chore from the time he arrived from work until 10 o'clock when it was bedtime in the Apple home. Although Peter avoided his chore as much as possible, it had to be done. And he did it with minimal complaint. After all, Chloe dealt with the messes and children all day without him, but he was relieved when his hours were up and even when morning came and it was time for another day at the factory.

Chloe said, "I wish you could spend more time at home with me and the babies."

Peter said, "Mila isn't such a baby, is she?"

Chloe cringed and fidgeted with her fingers. She said, "That's not the point, Peter. It's a lot of work taking care of an infant when you're sick."

Peter felt guilty for his daily work reprieve. He said, "I know, sugar plum, but we have to pay bills and diapers aren't cheap. Too bad they aren't very effective, either."

"Look, Pete. You wanted a boy, and it damn near killed me getting him to you. No complaints."

He felt properly chastised. "You're right, baby. I'm just being a grump. Forgive me?"

Releasing a groan of frustration, she rolled her eyes and said, "You're forgiven. You always are."

Peter reached his arm around her and pulled her tight against him, on the love seat, then gave her a kiss on the forehead. Smiling up at him, Chloe ran her fingers across his jawline. Feeling loved and comforted, she laid her head on his chest. Remembering how they used to spend hours holding each other, she smiled. The days before children, long gone. She said, "It's time for a shave, mister."

Mila felt lucky, listening to her parents—at four years old, she didn't have diaper duties. She adored the baby boy, and when he wasn't screaming she would beg to hold him. She followed as her parents made their way to their bedroom, then said, "Mommy, please. Can I hold my bubba? I washded my hands."

"Not right now, sweetie. He's sleeping."

"I won't wake him up, mommy, please!"

"No, Mila. How are you going to hold him without waking him?"

"I'll be gentle, Mommy."

"I don't think so, little girl. Every time you hold him you bump his head or some other nonsense."

Mila left the room upset, but Chloe wasn't about to risk a round of super lung frustration. She hadn't thought much of her dreams and worries since Barry was born, although she would get occasional chills when they crossed her mind. The screaming didn't rattle her much. She felt relieved he didn't have evil black eyes, and from what she could tell, he wasn't demonic.

Peter asked, "Have you had any more nightmares?"

Chloe replied with a tremble in her voice, "The last dream I had was when Barry was born. At least the last one I remember."

"Well, I don't know why I haven't asked you sooner.

What was it about?"

"It was dark, and I could hear him crying. I was alone in the darkness, except for his calls of frustration, but I couldn't see him. So I searched through the black and strange place until I found him. As soon as I picked him up—he stopped crying, and then I could see a purple glow coming from his eyes. I heard the voice again. It said 'I love you.' And I wasn't scared. I felt comforted."

"Why did you wait for me to ask? That sounds like something you would have shared on your own."

"I don't know. I did so much whining before, and I didn't know if the bad dreams would come back. Plus, I felt silly. What if that's what he was saying in all the dreams? I could never remember."

"In any case, sugar plum, as long as you're not having night terrors."

"No. Nothing scary lately. A lot of screaming and crying while I'm awake though."

Peter laughed and ran his fingers through his hair. He said, "Yeah, too bad it can't be like your dream and he shuts up when you pick him up."

Chloe squinted her eyes. She asked, "What did I tell you about complaining, mister?"

Peter raised his hands in an *I-don't-want-trouble* gesture. He said, "Just pointing out the obvious, baby. Don't hurt me."

Chloe laughed and rolled her eyes, replying, "Oh, I'll hurt you, mister. You just watch it is what you do."

In one swift move Peter grabbed his wife and kissed

her lips, hard and slow. He pulled away and held her at arm's length. He said, "I love you, sugar plum."

"I love you, too, babe."

Just then Barry woke and an enormous cry echoed through the bedroom.

4

Diaper problems only became worse as Barry grew older. When he learned how to pull the diaper off himself is when real trouble began. First in the crib, or wherever else he lay. Then he learned how to stand against objects or people and there was incident upon incident regarding soiled shoes, carpet, or anywhere else he could go. Before long he developed another habit that was equally disturbing: Barry became aggressive.

Mila screamed, "Mommy! Barry bit my hand again."

Barry bit and held on. Sometimes they would have to pry his little mouth off of things, or people. No one had any idea how he'd developed the habit. One day he just started randomly biting things and people with the clear intent of destroying them or harming the person. Chloe didn't know how to deal with her baby's assaults. She hadn't ever spanked Mila and she didn't want to start spanking Barry. She would ask Peter to do something.

"Peter, I'm so frustrated. I'll be doing the dishes, or laundry, and Barry will waddle up and hug my leg. The next thing I know he's gnawing on me. He almost bit Mila's finger off earlier today. You have to do something."

Peter suggested, "How about we get a muzzle for him."

Chloe slapped his chest. She said, "We're not putting a muzzle on him. Be serious. This isn't the time to joke. I'm not in the mood."

Peter grunted and ran his fingers through his hair. He said, "I'm not joking. I'm sure they make kid muzzles, don't they?"

Chloe shook her head and rolled her eyes. She said, "I don't know, Peter. Something about that just sounds wrong. Think of something else."

"I guess we could seek some professional help."

Chloe sighed and bit her lip. She said, "Things are getting worse, babe. Barry figured out that pulling Mila's hair makes her squeal. Now every time she gets close to him he tries to pull her hair or bite her. I just don't understand where all the aggression is coming from. Neither of us are aggressive people. I'm beginning to think our little rug rat might be evil."

Peter pulled Chloe close and looked out the kitchen window. She wrapped her arms around him and they stood silent and still for a short while. When he released her he picked up his *#1 Dad* coffee mug from the counter and took a slow sip. Setting it back down, he looked her in the eyes. He said, "I've got to get to work, sugar plum. Try not to let the little devil chew a hole in his sister while I'm gone and we'll figure this thing out later. If you want, you can get on the computer and see about some kind of therapist or some other specialist we can talk to about the problems." He showed a wicked but playful grin. He said, "Unless you want me to pick up a muzzle and some mitts on my way home from work."

Chloe screwed her face into a façade of disturbance. She said, "Sometimes I worry about you, too, mister. Are you sure he's not getting all this from you? You were probably a terror."

Peter picked up his coffee mug and took another sip. He said, "All boys are terrors, baby. He'll grow out of it. But still. We can get some opinions, if you want."

Later that day, while Mila was sitting on the floor watching television, Barry picked up the remote and threw it at her. Mila cried out, "Mommy! Barry's throwing things now. He hit me in the head."

Chloe rushed in and looked at the knot that Barry's projectile had produced. Infuriated, she looked at Barry. He was sitting on the floor with his usual look of agitation. Chloe picked him up, and he started screaming and fighting. She struggled to hold on to him. Sitting him down in his room kicking and screaming, she said, "Shut your mouth, little boy. You're going to stay in here and think about what you're doing."

Barry let out another shrill cry. Chloe said, "That's enough. Shut up."

She put a 'grip 'n twist' door knob cover on the inside door knob and closed the door. Barry screamed and hit the door from inside until he got tired. Chloe felt horrible locking him in the room. She waited for a little under an hour before letting him out to eat lunch.

Barry was quiet in his high chair while he ate his soup. He glared at his mother and sister until the meal was over. The awkward meal passed. Barry didn't make a single peep.

Excusing Mila and letting Barry down to wander, Chloe's stomach turned. Surprisingly, there were no disturbances or altercations while she cleaned the table and chairs. While in the kitchen, washing dishes, she thought to herself, *the room trick must have worked.* Barry hadn't made Mila scream or attacked either one of them in longer than he usually went without doing something aggressive. Then she began to wonder while soaping up a dish, *what is Barry doing?* She put the dish in the sink and went to check.

He wasn't in the living room, where Mila sat quietly watching a children's program. He wasn't in his room either. When she left his room she looked down the hall and saw Mila's door cracked open. Mila was supposed to keep her door shut so Barry couldn't get in. Chloe went to close it, but she decided to look inside. She found Barry. He was covered in feces, and so were Mila's walls, dolls and bed.

Chloe yelled, "Barry Pete Apple! What do you think you're doing?"

Barry looked at her with an evil scowl and spoke his first words. He said, "Sud up."

Chloe couldn't believe her ears. She asked, "What did you say?"

Barry twisted his face into an intense look of hatred

and screamed, "Sud up!"

When Peter returned home, Chloe had a list of behavioral specialists ready. Mila's first day of school was tomorrow and getting a doctor's appointment as quickly as possible was high on Chloe's priority list after the messy and aggressive day she'd had with the infamous toddler, Barry.

5

Peter left work early to be with Chloe when the day came to visit the psychiatrist. Mila was in school and the therapist's office wasn't far from the facility she attended. They'd scheduled the visit so as to allow them time to collect Mila afterwards. The appointment secretary seemed understanding and pleasant over the phone, but Chloe's nerves were rattled after trying to get Barry ready and loaded up to go. She was meeting Peter in the parking lot of the doctor's office and she was running late due to Barry's kicking and screaming, biting and yelling, "NO, NO, NO", (his second vocabulary word) all the way into his car seat.

She drove up the road with the fussy toddler in her ear. He'd already thrown everything he could reach in the car. Bottle spilled, stuffed animal in the floor board. The ugliest thoughts kept surfacing in Chloe's mind. Wanting to pull over and slap her belligerent son, she resisted the urge. Worse, darker thoughts invaded her once peaceful mind. She began to wish she hadn't given birth to Barry; she even disgusted herself with thoughts of abandoning him somewhere, or drowning him when he wouldn't co-operate with his evening bath. These thoughts would make Chloe sob uncontrollably at times.

Tears threatened to spill over and impede her ability to drive. Hoping she could make it to the doctor's office and Peter before having to pull over, she pressed on. Wiping her eyes with the sleeve of her shirt and accelerating the slightest bit over the speed limit, she was determined not to pull over, because she wasn't sure she would be able to control herself if she did. She couldn't trust herself to pull over now.

Pulling up in the newly paved parking lot, she spotted Peter's truck and parked next to it. Putting the car in park, she buried her face in her hands to cry. Peter was at her door tapping on the window within seconds. Barry's screaming in the back seat was all Chloe could hear. She felt relieved she hadn't worn makeup to the appointment. It would be ruined. Peter knocked on the glass harder. Lowering her hands, Chloe looked through the window at her patient and loving husband. Terrible thoughts cycled in her brain. She wondered if Peter had the same problem with diabolical thoughts. She wondered if he would understand what was happening to her. Wishing she could bring herself to ask him, she shuddered at the thought. She could ask him, but she was ashamed.

6

Dr. Payne's office was child-friendly and accommodating. Barry sat next to Peter on a padded placemat, colorfully decorated with 1, 2, 3's and A, B, C's. Chloe felt disgusted by how calm Barry was with his father. He barely gave her a break between screams and attacks. Poor Mila wouldn't get close enough to her brother to let him touch her for fear of his biting and hair-pulling. He sat still and quiet with Peter, rarely throwing a fit. Chloe didn't understand. She looked at him and longed to see innocence, but Barry wore a scowl. Even though he was just a toddler, to Chloe he seemed to harbor the spirit of hatred. Praying to see her son in a different light, Chloe felt helpless. She prayed for the ugly thoughts that plagued her to go away, along with her baby boy's behavior.

She turned her attention from Barry to Dr. Payne as the doctor entered the room. Chloe stood with her hand out. The Dr. reached out and took the nervous mother's hand in her own. Looking Chloe in the eye, the doctor smiled. She said, "It's good to meet you. Would it be okay if we took a seat over by my desk? I can feel your tension, maybe I can help, if it has to do with your son."

Chloe did feel tense. Her whole body felt wound tight. She was tense about her baby. After seeing Dr. Payne, she also felt tense about her husband. The doctor looked gorgeous, curved and younger than expected. Her green eyes and red hair a perfect combination, contrasting with chalk-white skin. The woman looked flawless. Resisting the urge to check where Peter's gaze landed, Chloe focused on the doctor. Hiding her self-consciousness in front of Gabriella Payne became an immediate task for Chloe. She let go of Dr. Payne's hand, and began to fidget. She said, "Y-Yes. Please. Let's sit. I would like that."

Taking a seat in the pink plush chair in front of the doctor's desk, Chloe resisted the urge once again to check on Peter. Dr. Payne asked, "Would you or your husband like anything to drink?"

Chloe glanced back at Peter and was relieved to see he wasn't gawking at the doctor. She asked, "Babe? Do you want something to drink?"

Peter smiled his gentle smile. He said, "Sure. I could use a water."

Chloe turned to face Dr. Payne, "Two waters would be fine."

The doctor asked, "Is it okay if I have juice brought in for Barry?"

Chloe said, "That's fine, nothing with sugar though. He gets worse when he has sugar."

Picking up the receiver on top of her desk, the doctor pushed a couple of numbers and after a short pause she spoke. She said, "Linda? Could you bring two adult waters in and a sugar free cranberry juice for a toddler? Yes, that's correct. Thank you."

Dr. Payne placed the receiver in the cradle and smiled. She said, "Refreshments are on the way. While we wait—tell me about yourself."

Chloe felt a nervous anxiety, she bit her lip. She asked, "What do you want to know?"

"Anything you wouldn't mind sharing. You can tell me about your childhood, adolescence, your daily routine. Anything you'd like."

"W-well, I'm not here to talk about me."

"Sure you are. We're here to talk about Barry. Most of what I'm going to learn about Barry's behavior, and the only way I'm going to know what's going on in his daily life, is through you. You are his voice. Unless he's some kind of child prodigy and has developed the kind of verbal skills it takes to tell me about his own life and family."

Chloe bite her lip again. Looking at her hands, she realized she was fidgeting. Dr. Payne said, "Talking about yourself to a psychiatrist doesn't come easy to most people, Mrs. Apple. I don't want you to think I'm here to judge you, because I'm not. I'm here to help find a solution to your problems."

Chloe nodded her head. She said, "I know. I'll try to be as cooperative as I can manage."

Dr. Payne smiled, her teeth reminding Chloe of how perfect the woman looked. The doctor said, "Great. Let's get started."

The office door opened and Linda entered with a couple of bottled waters and cranberry juice in a box with a straw. Her presence drew the attention of the room. She ventured to Peter and handed him a water. He thanked her, then she knelt down to give Barry his juice. Barry furrowed his brow and flung his arms out, yelling. "NO!"

Linda said, "Oh, my. Someone is cranky. Here, daddy."

She handed Peter the juice, with a smile. She said, "How about you hold this for the little one? He may get thirsty before the visit is over."

Peter accepted the drink. He said, "Thank you. He just came in from the heat, he'll change his mind."

Linda crossed the room and gave Chloe a water. Chloe thought to herself how Peter was always making excuses for Barry's behavior when he talked to strangers. It aggravated her. She knew he wasn't going to come out and say that Barry was a difficult child, but she wished he would. She didn't want to be the only one making complaints.

Linda left the room. Dr. Payne asked, "Where do you want to start, Chloe?"

Chloe said, "I don't know. Where should I?"

Dr. Payne asked, "How do you feel when you first wake up?"

"Well, I feel tired."

"Do you always feel tired?"

"Yes."

"I see."

Dr. Payne looked at a questionnaire she had on her desk. Chloe recognized the form, she had filled it out in the waiting room. Dr. Payne asked, "Do you take anything other than Tylenol?"

"No. I only take Tylenol when I get a headache or if I can't sleep."

"How often do you have trouble going to sleep?"

"Two or three times a week."

"I see. Do you take any other drugs that aren't listed? Narcotics?"

The hairs on the back of Chloe's neck stood up. She said, "No. I don't use illegal drugs. What are you suggesting?"

"Please, Mrs. Apple, these are the types of questions I ask all of my clients. I'm not here to judge you."

Chloe didn't hide her frustration. She said, "Yeah. You mentioned that. I don't see what your questions have to do with my eighteen-month-old baby's violent behavior."

"It has a lot to do with it, Mrs. Apple. A toddler with drug addicted parents may be neglected or abused, therefore causing the child to act out."

"Well, I can assure you that is not the case."

"Why are you so upset? If you did have a drug problem, it wouldn't be unusual. We could enroll you in some substance abuse courses. It would help improve the quality of your life and interactions with your children tremendously."

"Look little-miss-lip-gloss. I'm not a drug addict, and I don't appreciate the accusations."

Dr. Payne shifted in her seat. She said, "Maybe it's you who has the temper, Mrs. Apple. Your aggression is palpable."

Chloe's whole body began to shake. She said, "How dare you. I'm a loving mother."

"Do you ever lose your temper with Barry?"

Chloe looked back at Peter. He was busy with a stuffed animal, trying to keep Barry entertained. She knew he had to be hearing the conversation. If he was, he was doing a good job of playing the oblivious man in the background.

Chloe turned back to the doctor and rolled her eyes. She said, "No. I rarely lose my temper with anyone."

Dr. Payne studied Chloe's face for a moment. She said, "I find that hard to believe. It didn't take much to rattle your cage today. Do you ever hit your son?"

"No. Never. I've had just about enough of this. I'm not sitting through another second of your insults."

Chloe stood and turned to find Peter looking. He looked disturbed. She said, "Let's go, Peter."

Peter stood and picked up Barry. As they were heading out the office, the doctor called out. She said, "Chloe. If you're not willing to talk to me about what's going on, I think you should at least consider finding help elsewhere."

Chloe didn't look back. She left the doctor's office in a fury. Peter said, "I'll take Barry home, sugar plum. Are you gonna be okay?"

Chloe huffed and sat in her car. She said, "I'll be fine. I'm just so frustrated." Peter collected the car seat from the back. She slammed her door and left the parking lot with a screech.

7

Chloe washed dishes in silence while Peter put Mila and Barry to bed. She was lost in thought when he approached and put his hand on her shoulder. She almost dropped the plate she had been over-soaping. Throwing the dish in the sink, she spun around.

She said, "You shouldn't sneak up on me like that. What if I was holding a knife?"

Peter laughed, an easy going, calm sound. He said, "You probably would have dropped it in the sink, like you almost did with that plate."

Leaning in, he nibbled on her ear lobe. He asked, "Do you want to talk about it?"

Turning, she elbowed him gently in the ribs. She said, "There's nothing to talk about, mister."

He wrapped his arms around her from behind. He said, "There's plenty to talk about, sugar plum. I know you're frustrated if you didn't want to seethe and vent all evening. How about you leave the dishes for the night and we retire to the bedroom? You can cuss, stomp, do and say anything you'd like."

"No. I want to finish the dishes and take a shower, then we'll talk."

"Okay, sugar. If that's what you want. I don't want to go to bed until we've worked it all out, though."

"I bet, sneaky. You've got some kind of end game here."

"You bet I do. Peace of mind. I'd hate for you to murder the whole family in the middle of the night."

"Plus, you want to get lucky."

Peter kissed her neck and spoke with his lips on her skin. He said, "You know I do."

"Go get ready for bed, mister. I'll meet you in there."

8

Chloe entered the room and found it lit by candle light and Peter waiting for her, lying on the bed, looking like a happy little boy. Chloe pulled a nightgown from the dresser and gave him the *I'll-be-right-back* finger with a naughty look. She went to the master bathroom and turned the shower on. Peter stood and decided to follow her into the bathroom. That's when he heard the familiar cry of one Barry Apple. He picked up his robe from the bedside chair and headed in the direction of his son's room, hoping he could quell the toddler's restlessness before Chloe exited the shower.

Peter found Barry standing in his crib screaming with his face crimson. Everything from the inside of the crib was on the floor and as soon as Barry saw Peter he put his arms straight out to be picked up. Peter picked him up and stood him on the floor to fix his bed. Barry clung to Peter's leg while he cleaned the mess. When he had the bed made he picked Barry up and tried to put him back in the crib. Barry screamed and wouldn't release Peter's robe.

After several attempts to get Barry to calm down and lay in his crib, Peter decided to do the usual and bring him to the room with him and Chloe until he fell asleep again. It was a disappointment. Peter hoped to have a nice night with Chloe and calm her nerves. Now it was more of the same. The boy who seemed to terrorize his loving wife would be between them. As much as Peter loved his son, he wished Barry wasn't such a handful.

When he entered the room with Barry on his shoulder, Chloe was coming out of the bathroom. The look on her face said it all. Peter laid in the bed with his fussy son and Chloe left the room. Peter waited for her to return, but she didn't. He fell asleep with Barry.

In the morning, the alarm went off late. They had little obligation to do anything on Saturdays. It was odd to wake and find Chloe missing. Barry was awake staring at him. Peter knew his little terror was hungry.

He found Chloe and Mila in the kitchen. They were making pancakes, the smell of batter and cinnamon thick in the air. Chloe said, "Sit at the table, babe. I'll bring it to you."

Peter put Barry in his high chair and took a seat. It wasn't long before he had a stack of pancakes in front of him and Mila beaming at his side. Mila said, "I mixed the batter, Daddy! I put chocolate chips." Her smile warmed his heart.

"I see that, munchkin. They smell delicious."

"I bet they taste even better, Daddy. Taste them."

Peter poured syrup over the hot flap jacks and took a bite. He groaned in overly-exaggerated pleasure. He said, "Mmmm. These are delicious." He leaned over and gave Mila a kiss on the forehead. He said, "You did good, munchkin."

Chloe busied herself helping Barry with his breakfast. He was being surprisingly calm and willing to cooperate. He didn't refuse to let Chloe feed him and the morning was starting out peaceful. Peter knew he needed to talk to Chloe about the night before and the visit to the psychiatrist, but for now he enjoyed and basked in the household harmony. Barry even let Chloe clean him up without fuss when breakfast was over.

Once the children were finished with their meal and set free to watch cartoons and play, Peter had his chance to talk to Chloe alone. While helping gather dishes and wiping the table, he struck up the conversation he knew he should have, with a question.

"What exactly happened at the doctor's office yesterday?"

"Peter, I don't want to talk about it."

Peter went to the sink to help Chloe wash dishes. He said, "I think we should talk about it. You were so frustrated, and I want to help."

Chloe let the dish in her hands slide back into the soapy water. She said, "That woman was insinuating I'm a bad mother."

"Are you sure she wasn't just ruling things out? I heard you get upset. You made a comment about her lip gloss."

Chloe threw her dish towel on the counter. She asked, "Are you taking her side?"

"Whoa, sugar plum. I'm always on your side. You

know that, right?"

He moved toward her with his arms out for a hug. She turned and stormed out of the kitchen. The conversation hadn't gone the way he'd expected. He decided to finish the dishes and give her a chance to cool off.

Before he finished the dishes the home phone rang. Chloe was in the bedroom and she wasn't about to pick up. Peter dried his hands and looked at the caller ID. It was one of Chloe's friends from high school. It always put her in a good mood when she talked to Grace, and Peter hoped a call from her friend would bring Chloe out of the funk. He picked up before the call was lost.

"Hello?"

"Peter? Is Chloe in?"

"Yeah. Let me get her for you. She'll be happy to hear your voice, Grace. Give me a second."

"Okay. I'll hold."

Peter went to the bedroom and found Chloe face down in a pillow. He said, "Grace is on the line, sugar."

"Tell her I'll call her back. I don't want to talk right now."

Peter went to sit beside her and began rubbing her back. He said, "C'mon, sugar. It's your best friend. It'll make you feel better if you talk to her."

"Bring me the phone."

Peter left the room and returned quickly. He handed the phone to Chloe. She rolled over on her back and put the receiver to her ear. Peter left the room.

Grace asked, "Is everything okay, short stuff?"

"Yeah. I'm just a little down and out."

"How long has it been since we've seen each other?"

"Since Darla and Barry were about two months old."

"I know. Almost a year and a half. Can you believe it?"

"Maybe I can talk Peter into a trip to see you sometime, soon."

"That would be nice. I have some news for you."

"Oh?"

"I'm in town! I could come see you this afternoon if you'd like."

"This better not be a joke, Grace. I don't think I could handle anymore disappointment right now."

"It's not a joke, Chloe. I'm at a motel in town right now. Kevin wanted to visit his mother. She's really sick."

"I'm sorry to hear that."

"I know. It's so sad. She's been diagnosed with a brain tumor. She doesn't have long to live."

"That's horrible."

In light of the news Chloe felt foolish wallowing in her own sorrows. Grace said, "We're going to see her in another hour or so, then we can come visit, if that's okay."

"Of course it is. I'll be looking forward to it."

9

Grace arrived with Kevin and Darla late in the afternoon. Chloe felt overjoyed to be at the door greeting her friend whom she loved so much; Grace leaned over Chloe and embraced her. The girls had made their plans earlier by phone: They were to have dinner together and some girl time afterwards. The daddies would watch the little ones while the ladies sat on the porch, sipped wine and caught up with one another.

Kevin stood at the door stoop holding Darla while the women embraced and then Chloe excitedly ushered the Austin family into the Apple home. Peter and Kevin had never been close. They weren't friends in high school. They probably wouldn't be speaking now, if it weren't for their wives. It's not that they were mortal enemies, it wasn't that serious. They had different ways of doing things, and different attitudes toward life and the way people should be treated. Kevin had been the school bully, and the only fight he and Peter ever had was over a skinny kid Kevin considered a nerd and decided to beat on in the locker room showers.

Peter was always the type to take up for others. Kevin was the type to knock others down. After the high school scuffle, Peter would just as soon have never spoken to Kevin again. The worst part about the situation was that Peter had been labeled some kind of monster because of the beating he gave Kevin. Although he only fought when provoked, Peter was pretty damn good at boxing. On the day he fought Kevin, he was in a rage. He kept on beating him even after Kevin fell unconscious. It took several teachers to wrestle Peter to the ground, and Kevin was hospitalized for several days afterward. It didn't help when Kevin returned to school visibly black and blue and looking as though he'd been hit by a truck. On top of that, he behaved timidly the rest of the year, and this seemed to garner sympathy for Kevin and disdain for Peter.

During college, Kevin and Chloe's best friend Grace became an item. They got married, and little Darla was born in the same month as Barry, leading Peter's rival right to his doorstep. Chloe knew the history between the two men and so did Grace. They all had attended the same high school and Kevin's beating was no secret. The papers had labeled Peter a monster and Kevin played the victim well.

Peter thought about what he'd say to Kevin now. When Grace came home to have Darla, Peter hadn't made any attempt to make amends. Seeing Kevin hold his daughter and enter the home brought back a plethora of memories long forgotten. Peter knew at a time like the present it would be wrong to be anything but polite.

Chloe said to Grace, "I've been waiting so long to spend time with you. I can't believe you're finally here."

Grace was happy to see Chloe but the sadness in Grace's eyes betrayed the women's feelings. Chloe could always read her. She had a lot going on and apparently, Kevin's grief regarding his mother was taking its toll on her. Grace smiled an unnatural smile. She said, "I hope we're not intruding."

Chloe reassured her with another embrace. She said, "Don't be silly. You could never be intruding in my house. Are you thirsty? I made sweet tea."

"Sure." Grace turned to Kevin. She asked, "Are you thirsty, dear?"

Kevin replied, "My tongue is sticking to the roof of my mouth. Sweet tea sounds great."

Chloe reached out to hold Darla. Kevin handed over his daughter and Chloe started gushing over the toddler. She turned to Peter smiling. She asked, "Would you mind getting the refreshments, babe? I'm going to go get Darla settled in with the kids. I want to see if Barry will play well with her."

"No problem, sugar. I'll bring a glass to you."

Chloe and Grace left the foyer with Darla. Peter looked at Kevin, standing in the entryway alone. He couldn't think of anything to say to him. He was about to turn around and go to the kitchen without a word, then Kevin spoke.

"I'm sorry about the whole school incident. You and I both know it was my fault, and I've never really had the opportunity to apologize. I guess you probably hate my guts."

Peter was caught off guard. He'd spent so long trying to think of something to say that would keep the evening civil, and here was Kevin, apologizing. Peter said, "They made me out to be some kind of animal over the way I acted."

"I know. I kept talking shit until I blacked out. I'm surprised you didn't kill me after some of the things I said."

Peter felt an apprehension. He wasn't sure he should let Kevin Austin into his life. Even for an evening. Kevin had bullied and manipulated his way through life for all the years Peter had known him. It was hard to comprehend real change in someone you hadn't spent time with in years. It was difficult to believe that Kevin had seen the error of his ways, or somehow had decided to admit he was wrong, after all these years, and mean it.

Peter took in Kevin's appearance. The man was gaunt. Black circles underneath his eyes. The weary look of a traveler through hell and back. His shirt was wrinkled and there were hints of his pain everywhere. Peter thought to himself, *maybe Kevin made changes*. He knew that he himself wasn't the same person that he was in high school.

Peter said, "Let's get the drinks."

Kevin asked, "Do you accept my apology?"

Peter gave it a second's thought, and said, "I accept you, Kevin. We've all done things we would do differently today. Don't give me any more reasons to dislike you; I can leave the past in the past."

10

The evening proceeded nicely; Chloe and Grace now sat on the porch with wine glasses in hand. The night air felt cool and the wind's soft touch blew the women's hair about. They were a little tipsy after a couple of glasses and their worries and troubles were yet to be mentioned. Only talking of the good times, laughing, smiling at one another. Then, Grace's demeanor turned dark.

Grace said, "I think I want a divorce."

Chloe looked into the shallow pool of liquid left in her glass, then to Grace. She asked, "Is it that bad?"

"Yes. He's mean. He's always saying mean things to me."

Chloe's stomach churned at the tone of Grace's voice. Grace frowned, and sadness marked the moment. Chloe asked, "Have you been thinking this way long?"

A tear escaped Grace's eye and rolled down her tan cheek. Her voice trembled as she said, "He's such a jerk. I hate him. But now his mother's dying and it makes it that much harder to leave. What kind of person would I be to leave at a time like this?"

Chloe was searching for the right thing to say. Grace continued, "He breaks things all the time. Not just his things, either. He breaks my stuff. Even Darla's things. I can't stand it. He hasn't hit me yet, but he's always saying he should kick my ass. I know he's going to do it one day. I see it in his eyes."

Chloe shuddered—her friend's words were a shock to her ears. Grace hadn't revealed any of this in their frequent phone conversations over the past eighteen months. She always seemed up-beat. Most of their conversations were about the babies and mom life. She couldn't have guessed things at home were such a miserable wreck.

Having her dear friend here disclosing an abusive home life brought thoughts of Chloe's own abusive background to the forefront. Living with her physically abusive stepfather, even after her own mother disappeared without a trace. She had been his ragdoll, a human punching bag. She never even attempted telling anyone of her troubles. Too afraid she would be placed in foster care and moved around the country. Away from the love of her life, Peter. She was overcome with relief the day her tormentor died in a twisted mess of steel, driving drunk.

Chloe felt sick inside and her fear for her friend was palpable. Grace said, "I don't mean to worry you, Chloe. I'm sorry."

"Don't be sorry, Grace. That's absurd. I'm your friend and I want to help. Even if all you want me to do is listen."

"That's all I need. I just had to get it off my chest. It's like he's sucking the life out of me. When he's around I feel like I can barely breathe. Do you ever get that feeling?"

Chloe knew the feeling all too well. But she didn't feel up to opening her wounds at the moment, even though she knew she could relate and relay the terror. She took a deep breath. She said, "He's a bully, Grace. He always was a bully. I know what it's like to be bullied and it feels like hell. I can imagine what it must be like for you."

Grace asked, "Do you think it would be wrong if I left him now? While his mom's dying?"

"If you feel like he might do something to you, maybe it's best you leave." Chloe felt an apprehension as soon as the words left her mouth. She was trying to avoid making any kind of statement that would push Grace in either direction.

Chloe continued, "The choice is yours, Grace. You know what's best for you. No one can make the decision but you."

The screen door opened and Kevin stepped out on the porch. Chloe straightened in her chair and Grace wiped the lone tear-streak.

Kevin didn't seem to sense anything wrong. He said, "It's getting late, Gracie. I'm getting Darla ready to go."

Grace put her right hand to her mouth and began to chew her index fingernail. She spoke while she gnawed away. She asked, "Could we stay a little longer? I'm still visiting."

Kevin visibly tensed. He said, "I'm sure you could visit all night, Grace. Everything isn't about you though, is it? Darla is tired and so am I. Now get your hand out of your mouth and get ready. I'm going to the bathroom and when I come out I expect to be walking out the front door with you in tow. Understood?"

11

Chloe and Grace went inside and found Peter on the couch watching television. Barry, Mila and Darla were on the floor playing with building blocks. The women observed the children for a moment. Chloe couldn't believe how well behaved Barry had been all day, and how well he was playing with Darla.

Chloe grasped Grace's hand. She said, "I wish you didn't have to leave."

Grace replied, "I wish I didn't have to either." Then a smile spread wide across Grace's face.

She said, "Look, Chloe! He's going to kiss her."

Chloe looked at her son leaning towards Darla. The boy didn't kiss the girl, he bit. He bit hard, clamping down like a Pitbull on prey. Darla shrieked with the kind of cry that could turn the paint on the walls different colors.

Chloe squeezed Grace's hand and Peter reacted with a lunge towards the toddlers. Before he could get to his feet, Kevin appeared from the hallway and was on top of the two interlocked children. He immediately began swatting Barry's head to get him to release his bite. Release Barry did, with a loud wail due to the adult's assault.

Peter was on his feet and nearly pushed Kevin down reaching his son. He looked Kevin in the eyes with a flesh curling stare. He asked, "Who the fuck do you think you are? You think you can come in my house and hit my son?"

Peter went to Chloe and tried handing her Barry. Chloe kept her grip on Grace's hand and shook her head. She knew if she took Barry from her husband's embrace, he would attack the man who made him cry. She could envision Kevin pressing charges, sending her loving husband, Barry's protective father, to jail.

Peter's frustration and anger filled the small room. The intense situation had all the qualities of what could grow into epic disaster. Kevin put his hands up in an— I don't want trouble—gesture. He said, "We just want to leave." He looked at Grace with a gleam in his eyes. He said, "Get your things and meet me in the car." Then he picked Darla up from the floor and headed for the front door.

Tears flowed from Grace and Chloe's eyes. The two women embraced and Grace began gathering her things. Chloe said, "I don't know what to say, Grace. This ended so badly." She felt terrible about what Barry had done.

Grace replied, "Kevin shouldn't have hit your baby. I'm the one that should be saying sorry."

Peter interjected, "You have nothing to be sorry about. He's a grown man. You aren't responsible for his actions."

When Grace left, Chloe was in a worse mood than she had been all week. She knew she wouldn't be seeing her friend again any time soon. Poor Darla's cheek was bleeding and would definitely bruise. After Grace confided in her, she also knew things were going to be that much more hectic for her at home.

12

Several months had passed since Chloe had last heard from her friend Grace. She hadn't answered her cell phone or responded to emails. A "phone-has-been-disconnected" message played in her ear when she called the house phone. Chloe had even sent a letter to her friend's address: It came back to her unopened, with a "return-to-sender" message stamped upon the envelope.

She asked Peter, "Why do you think Grace is avoiding talking to me?"

"I don't know, sugar plum. She's probably going through hell with that bastard husband of hers. I doubt it has anything to do with you."

"It's not like her, though. We talked once or twice a week since she moved away. I'm really starting to worry."

Peter could see how concerned Chloe was and it hurt his heart. He said, "I'll look up Kevin's number today and reach him however I can. Maybe I can get some answers."

Chloe was elated, "You'd do that for me, babe?"

"You bet. I've got to get to work, but on my lunch

break I'll do the research."

Chloe kissed Peter before continuing her morning routine. Peter finished his coffee and headed out the door.

Peter's work load wasn't too stressful as a general rule, but the one-hour lunch break always came as a relief. When it arrived, Peter used the company's Wi-Fi and began a search on Kevin Austin. He found Kevin's place of work, home phone, and cellular. There wasn't much time left for a phone call, but Peter wrote the numbers down and planned to make the calls as soon as he punched out for the day.

Meanwhile, Chloe busied herself at home with Barry. He was approaching his second birthday and had become more mischievous by the day. He spent his time walking or running around the house tearing anything off the walls that he could reach. Curtains and blinds couldn't stay up for more than a couple of hours. He had to be watched constantly or something would be broken. Figurines, unattended cordless phones and plates—nothing was safe from Barry's perpetual onslaught.

The end of the work day came right on schedule. No overtime. Another day gone. Peter sat in his truck and started it, to let the air-conditioner blow. It was always a welcome relief after the factory. He looked forward to being home with the person he liked to spend his time with most. He didn't want to talk to Kevin, but if it would make the woman he adored happy, he would do it willingly.

He tried the house phone first. The operator's message came on immediately, the number had been disconnected as he expected. He hung up and tried the cell phone next. After two short rings there was an answer. It sounded like Kevin.

The man said, "Hello?"

Peter asked, "Is this Kevin Austin?"

The man asked, "Who is this? If you're selling something I'm not interested."

"I'm not selling anything. I'm calling about Grace."

The man's voice became stressed. He said, "Look. If you're looking for something new to the story, I'll tell you like I told the rest of the reporters, police and everyone else who keeps asking. I don't know where she is, okay? I came home and she was gone. Left me and my daughter without a word, letter or any other kind of common courtesy. I'd appreciate it if you didn't call me anymore. I'm trying to get on with my life."

Without another word the line went dead. Peter placed his phone on the dashboard and paused a second to absorb all that Kevin had just disclosed. He contemplated calling back and clarifying who he was. After some consideration, he thought it would be best to call back from home, while Chloe was with him, if she wanted to.

The ride home seemed to take longer than usual with the heavy news he now had weighing on his mind. He worried about how such a revelation might affect Chloe. He remembered how it was when her mother had gone missing. She withdrew from everything back then, quitting the cheer squad and even missing school regularly. He hated that he was going to have to potentially crush her world.

13

When Peter entered his home he was greeted by Mila first. She ran to him and wrapped herself around his left leg. She said, "Daddy! I'm so glad you're home."

Peter bent over and lifted her up, pulling her in with a tight embrace. He said, "I'm glad to be home, munchkin."

Chloe and Barry appeared in the foyer and he was surrounded by his loving family. Even Barry became excited and happy when his father came in from work. It was Peter's favorite part of the day. Nothing could compare to the feeling of such a tremendous greeting. It bothered him that soon he would be giving bad news to his beautiful, smiling wife.

With a kiss on the cheek, Chloe said, "Dinner's on the table, babe." She took Mila and turned, heading for the dining area.

Picking Barry up, Peter followed. He strapped Barry into the high chair and went to the bathroom to wash his hands. When he came back Chloe had made him a plate and was serving fried chicken, green beans and mashed potatoes to the children. It smelled great. When Peter took his seat, Chloe began passing him bowls of delicious smelling foods. He already had several pieces of chicken thanks to his loving wife and he heaped more green beans and potatoes on his plate.

They said a prayer over the food and Peter immediately began putting a dent in the bounty before him. He was hoping that Chloe wouldn't ask him about Grace or the call he was supposed to make at work until later. Chloe asked, "How was your day, babe?"

Peter did his best to elaborate on everything he could. He said, "It went well. Jordan is still out on sick leave so my work load is practically doubled. But maybe I'll get a raise with all the extra work. My supervisor seemed to notice how much I'm getting done. He complimented me today."

"That's good, babe. I'm proud of you. Did you get around to what I asked you about this morning?"

A lump rose in Peter's throat. He knew it wasn't the type of conversation he wanted to have in front of the children. Peter said, "Let's wait until after dinner, sugar."

A puzzled and worried look drew over Chloe's face. The meal was close to over and the seconds and minutes seemed to speed up for Peter. He hated that he had to tell Chloe what he'd discovered. He contemplated various ways of telling what Kevin said over the phone. He tried desperately to figure out a way to put it that wouldn't worry her worse than she already was.

When the kids were washed up and the table was cleared, Peter joined Chloe at the sink to help with the dishes. Chloe asked, "Did you get ahold of Kevin?"

"I did."

"Well?

"He didn't know it was me on the phone."

Chloe giggled. She asked, "Did you lie about who you were?"

"No. Not exactly."

Chloe slapped Peter with her dish rag. She said, "Out with it, mister. All this suspense is wearing on my nerves."

Peter took a deep breath and decided to be direct. He said, "He thought I was a reporter. Apparently reporters and police have been calling about Grace. She's missing, Chloe."

Chloe dropped the dish she was holding in the sink. It landed with a crash as it broke.

14

Three years had now passed since Chloe had learned of Grace's disappearance and there'd been no trace of her to be found. Chloe never let go of the thought that her friend was still alive, although her gut told her that Kevin had done something horrible to her. Getting Barry ready for his first day of school, she couldn't help but think of Darla starting her first day without her mother. Chloe had contacted the police department in Chicago and everyone else she could think of who might give her some answers. The answers were all consistent, no body, no crime.

She put Barry's shoes on and did her best to get him and Mila in the car without too much fuss. To her amazement, the children were in the car in record time buckled and quiet. The ride to the school was surprisingly uneventful. It didn't calm Chloe's nerves, though.

Barry hadn't spent much time around other children and it was worrying Chloe that he might not get along with the other students. He didn't bite nearly as much, but he still liked to hit people, throw and destroy things. They discussed home schooling him, but she'd already spent so much time at home. It seemed imperative to give public school a chance. She wanted him to do well. Chloe had a strong and growing desire to go back to work outside the home for a change, and today she would finally do just that.

Chloe prayed as she entered the grade school classroom. She prayed that Barry wouldn't cause too big a scene when she tried to leave him with the teacher. They entered the room of toddlers, the teacher on the far side, busy with another parent. Regretting not having put him in kindergarten the previous year, she braced herself for this experience. When the parent who'd been talking to the teacher tried to leave, their little girl put up a fuss. Looking down at Barry, Chloe wondered how he was going to react to her leaving him. Peter had been talking to him, telling him about school and how he was going to make so many new friends.

Barry watched the children run around the room and play with toys. He didn't seem apprehensive or frightened at all. The teacher approached with a smile. She said, "I'm Mrs. Marsh." She leaned over at eye level to Barry. She asked, "Who's this little man?"

Chloe was surprised and relieved to see Barry smile at his new teacher. Chloe said, "This is Barry Apple, and it's his first time in a classroom."

Mrs. Marsh offered her hand and Barry took it. Chloe was glad to see that his teacher had such a gentle way with children. It eased her mind in a small way. There were still the other children and activities he would be expected to participate in.

Chloe took in the room one last time before she was to attempt her exit. The colorful walls, shoe bins and A, B, C's along with 1, 2, 3's. An overall cheerful atmosphere, it was all reassuring. Mrs. Marsh stood upright. She said, "Mrs. Apple, we'll be seeing you at about three o'clock." Then she looked down at Barry. She said, "Say goodbye to mommy, Barry."

Chloe thought how innocent Barry looked holding his teachers hand, then he flipped the bird. Chloe's eyes became golf balls. Her insides turned a flip. She looked at Mrs. Marsh and began fidgeting. She said, "I don't know where he learned that." She asked Barry, "Where did you learn that?"

He said, "A movie."

Chloe was beet-red embarrassed, she apologized to Mrs. Marsh. Mrs. Marsh said, "They see and learn all kinds of things—they copycat, Mrs. Apple. With everything they show in movies now days, it's a chore to quell the deviance."

She knelt to talk to Barry. She said, "That's an inappropriate gesture here, Little Mr. Apple. Do you understand?"

To Chloe's amazement Barry nodded his head acknowledging he understood. Almost like he felt remorse for the obscene gesture. Chloe's faith in Mrs. Marsh was growing. All she needed to do now was make her exit.

Chloe said, "I'll be here at three to pick him up then."

Mrs. Marsh stood and smiled. She said, "Very well,

Mrs. Apple. We'll see you at three."

Chloe turned to leave and Barry didn't make a peep. Outside the classroom door it became reality, Barry was spending his first day at school and away from her. An overwhelming joy rose inside as she stepped out of the building. She was finally going back to work! After five years of strictly family-life, it was time to step out into the adult world of labor. She couldn't have been happier.

15

Chloe pulled into the bakery's parking lot and checked her make-up in the rear-view mirror. Her feeling of joy turned into a feeling of anxiety. She wondered how many new people were staffed. It worried her thinking about whether she would get along with everyone and if her job was going to be the same. Taking a deep breath, she calmed herself with positive affirmations 'Everyone loves me. I'm good at any task given. I'm going to do great'. Then she exited her vehicle and headed inside.

The bakery smelled delicious. She visited frequently enough, and now she was working a half shift. Julissa was a rounded, rosy-cheeked, up-beat manager. She met Chloe at the door, arms wide, with an enormous smile. Chloe was enveloped in her boss's tight embrace and warm welcome.

Julissa said, "It's so good to have you back, Chloe. We've all missed you."

Chloe thanked her. She asked, "What will I be doing?"

"No worries, dear. We're going to keep you busy.

Your position as head-baker has been filled of course, but for now you can help with yeast-prep and whatever else needs to be done, you know the ropes."

Chloe let a nervous laugh escape. She said, "If I can remember after all these years."

Julissa said, "Oh, honey, you'll be fine."

Julissa walked with Chloe to the back and the women that already knew her acted indifferent. She was introduced to the three women she had yet to meet. Two of them were polite but somewhat passive. The third took an interest in getting to know Chloe, exhibiting the type of charisma and beauty that made the woman both attractive and intimidating. The gorgeous brunette had a dazzling smile with picture perfect teeth. Her hazel eyes were focused and noticeably observant. She was not shy about taking a long look at her surroundings or people in them. These things were automatically obvious to Chloe.

She was introduced as Rebecca; the woman Chloe would be spending the day rolling dough with. Rebecca said, "You're really pretty. It's hard to believe you have children with your figure."

Rebecca's interest in her appearance made Chloe uncomfortable, but she wasn't the first to make comments like that about her. Peter said things like that all the time. It was just strange coming from someone who seemed like the definition of physical perfection. For someone who wasn't shy about saying what she thinks or pointing out physical observations, Rebecca spoke very softly. Her tone was sensual and seductive.

Chloe found herself attracted to her and it made her even more uncomfortable.

Chloe replied, "Thank you. You're pretty, too. What kind of Asian are you?"

A curious look in Rebecca's eyes made Chloe immediately regret her question. Rebecca said, "I'm the Asian type of Asian. Does it matter? I was raised by my father, he's white."

Chloe felt embarrassed. She said, "I didn't mean to offend you. I'm just a curious person, I guess." She bit her lip.

Rebecca squinted. She said, "Beautiful. I'm a curious person, also." She smiled, and somehow this reminded Chloe of a tiger she'd seen in photographs. Rebecca said, "I'm half Vietnamese, half Italian."

Chloe began fidgeting; she realized it and abruptly stopped. She said, "I'm German and Italian. Really just an American. Texan. I'm a mutt."

Rebecca laughed, an intoxicating sound. She said, "You're not alone. Most people are. I can be spotted quickly, though. You're lucky, you blend better."

Chloe released a nervous laugh. She said, "It must not be all bad, right? I mean, you have such an exotic look. Do you have children?"

Rebecca looked at her with that curious spark in her eyes. She said, "I'm wondering if that's all there is to your life."

Chloe was taken back and found herself becoming defensive; she spoke out of the side of her mouth. She said, "There's plenty to my life."

Rebecca showed another wicked smile. She said, "I'd like to hear about it."

Chloe replied, "How about some other time?"

"I'd like that, Chloe. Get to know each other better."

Chloe began to blush. She was going to have to figure out how to fill in the blanks. Saying that her life consisted of much more than the children was a bold-faced lie, all she'd been doing before starting her job again was taking care of Barry and Mila. Now she felt embarrassed. She began kneading dough.

Rebecca said, "No."

Chloe was confused. She asked, "No, what?

"I don't have children."

Before leaving to pick Barry and Mila up, Chloe told Rebecca they would make plans to get together. They exchanged numbers and Chloe promised to let her know what Peter said about her having drinks in the evening. Chloe beamed; having someone invite her out felt exciting. It also made her nervous.

16

Chloe pulled close to the school and found a parking space. She exited the car and crossed the street onto the lawn. When the bell rang, children began to flood from the doorways. Chloe walked through the rushing waves of students to where the first grade class let out.

It wasn't long before the smaller kids' classes began pouring through the doorways, teachers gathering and herding their little students like shepherds watching over their flocks. It was hard for Chloe to fathom the kind of patience and understanding it took to teach and look after a class of first graders. She thought to herself how extraordinary the teachers were.

She spotted Mrs. Marsh with Barry at her side. Mrs. Marsh noticed her simultaneously. When Chloe approached she could see Barry wasn't in a good mood. He was wearing his signature scowl. Mrs. Marsh waved as Chloe closed the gap. Chloe braced herself for bad news.

Mrs. Marsh asked, "How was your day, Mrs. Apple?"

Chloe was caught off guard by the question. She

said, "It was good. I'm glad to be back at work."

"I'm happy to hear it." Her eyes wandered over the crowd. She continued, "Little Mr. Apple had a good day, also." She looked at Barry and smiled. She said, "Tell your mommy about your day when you get home, Barry."

Barry said, "If I want."

Mrs. Marsh said, "Don't you want to share all the activities with your family?"

He said, "I don't care."

Mrs. Marsh shook her head. She said, "Very well, Little Mr. Apple. Suit yourself."

She looked at Chloe. She said, "Everything went fine. He has a bit of a mouth and exhibits violent tendencies, but it's not uncommon. Although there is something that concerns me."

Chloe knew there would be something. Mrs. Marsh said, "Barry fell asleep in class, and when I tried to wake him, he attempted to bite me. It was a struggle to keep him from sinking his teeth into me. Then, he began throwing things. We had to take him out of the classroom for a short period."

Chloe felt like her face was going green. Mrs. Marsh asked, "Could it be possible that he needs some adjustments to his sleeping schedule?"

Chloe wasn't sure how to have the conversation she was now engaged in. Barry had practically no sleeping schedule. He refused to be put to bed when directed to. He would get up and play in his room and had even been found wandering the house or watching television while everyone slept.

Chloe said, "I'll do what I can to see that he gets more sleep. He must have been having some kind of wild dream to wake up acting like he did."

Mrs. Marsh said, "Yes, well, if he actually bites or becomes physically aggressive with staff or students we will have to notify you and it's possible he will need to be picked up."

The words coming from Mrs. Marsh's mouth were a sobering reality. Barry was a biter, amongst other things. Sooner or later she knew that Barry's ugliness would surface its diabolical head. Chloe had little faith that he could make it through the school year without incident. It was just a matter of time.

Chloe said, "I understand."

She took Barry by the hand, but he pulled away. It was an embarrassing spectacle in front of the teacher. Barry said, "I don't have to hold your hand to walk. I'm not a baby."

Chloe asked, "Are you going to follow me? We've got to go pick up your sister."

Barry scowled. He said, "I'll follow. I'm ready to go home."

"We're going home after we get your sister."

They walked away, towards the side of the school where Mila could be found. It didn't take long to pick her out of the crowd. She liked wearing bright colors and ribbons in her hair. She was talking with some of her friends from the year before. When she spotted her mother and brother walking up, a huge smile stretched across her little face. Mila smiling was almost a constant thing. She loved her family and she was never scared to show it in public or private. She ran to her mother and began calling to her friends to meet her baby brother.

Mila said, "Barry, meet Sandra and Veronica."

Veronica giggled. She said, "Hello, Barry. You're really cute."

Barry said, "You're ugly," his eyebrows close-knit in a mean mug.

The girls looked at each other incredulously. Mila put her hand on her friend's arm. She said, "He hates being called cute."

The girls giggled in unison. Mila said, "I'll see y'all tomorrow." The girls blew Barry kisses and hugged Mila.

In the car, Chloe adjusted the rear-view so that she could see Barry in the back seat. She could read hatred on the young boy's face. He wasn't abused at home and it hurt her that he was the way he was. She didn't realize she had been staring when he noticed her looking. He scowled at her in the mirror.

Chloe asked, "Why are you such an angry child, sweetie? It doesn't make sense."

Barry said, "You're a stupid-head." Then he looked out the window to ignore her.

Chloe wanted to cry. She thought to herself that Barry wouldn't ever be a normal child. She liked to fantasize he would become a positive, productive adult. Every time he said something mean, or did something violent, it dashed Chloe's dream that much more. He had a problem with anyone looking at him for more than a second. It caused fights between him and Mila all the time. His attitude was frustrating to everyone in his life, except Peter. Chloe couldn't understand. It was hard not to envision disaster when thinking of all his antics.

Mila was the opposite of her little brother. She was somewhat shy, but always courteous with new people, and a blessing to those who knew her. She also dealt with a good deal of Barry's abuse without saying a word. Unless she was bleeding and needed a bandage, she wouldn't even call attention to anything he did, on purpose. She didn't like getting him in trouble. Mila believed he couldn't help the way he was, and she loved him more every day.

When Chloe pulled away from her parking space, Mila twisted in the front seat to look back at him. She asked, "How was your first day, boo-boo?"

Barry said, "I din-nit like it."

Mila asked, "Why not, boo-boo? Didn't you make friends?"

Barry was done talking. He turned to stare out the window, back into his own world. Chloe took the silent moment to ask Mila how her day was. Mila was excited to talk about it. She said, "It was great. Sandra went to Disney world and Veronica spent the summer with her dad. My teacher is really nice and didn't give us any homework. We're all in some of the same classes, too."

Barry began making loud fart noises with his mouth. The girls smiled at each other and rolled their eyes.

Chloe turned the radio up to drown out the symphony of mouth-made flatulence. When they arrived home, Barry was still making the noises. It wasn't an unusual occurrence for him to be intentionally obnoxious, and the girls were glad the trip was over.

Once inside Chloe wasted no time kicking into gear. She made sure the kids were comfortable, made them a snack, and started preparing to cook the evening meal. She had enjoyed her day, and she wanted her new found freedom to last. Praying Barry didn't begin gnawing on any teachers or students, she busied herself in the kitchen.

17

When Peter arrived home, dinner was ready. The family sat at the round table with the aroma of spaghetti, meatballs and garlic-bread filling the air. They bowed their heads and Peter said a short prayer before Chloe served the children, then passed the bowls for Peter to serve himself. He knew Chloe wanted to talk about her day. He asked, "How did everything go at the bakery, sugar plum?"

Chloe smiled and he could see she was pleased with the inquiry. She said, "It went better than I expected. I had so much anxiety, but it was nice when I got started. Everyone says they missed me. Rita isn't there anymore, but I think I made a new friend out of one of the new girls."

Peter felt happy hearing Chloe had enjoyed her day and made a new friend. She continued, "The new girl's name is Rebecca. She wanted to know if I could go out for drinks with her sometime."

She began eating with haste to cover up how nervous the question made her, but it only served to make her anxiety obvious to Peter. He spoke in a joking tone. He said, "You mean you want to leave me here, alone, with these monsters?" He laughed.

Chloe said, "Hey, mister. I'm always here, alone, with these 'monsters'."

Mila said, "Mom, dad—I'm right here."

Peter turned to Mila. He said, "Yes you are, little monster. Tell me how your day was."

"It was great. I got to see Sandra and Veronica again."

Peter turned to Barry. He asked, "How was your day, buddy? Did you like your class?"

Barry replied, "I din-nit like it."

"Why not? Wasn't your teacher nice?"

"She was a doo-doo head. She wouldn't leave me alone."

Peter asked, "What were you doing?"

"I was trying to sleep and she wouldn't let me. So I din-nit like her."

Peter said, "You go to school to learn, not sleep, son. You probably would have fun if you paid attention."

Barry was visibly displeased with his father's comments. He began giving everyone dirty looks, then in a quick motion, he pushed his plate to the floor. It landed with a loud crash, glass and food spilling beside him and under the table. Following was the clank of silverware on plates. Mila stared at her brother in awe.

Peter said, "Go to your room, Barry Pete Apple."

Barry stared defiantly for a moment, then left the table. It was moments like this that Peter and Chloe considered taking up physical punishment. Barry hadn't suffered a stern paddling before, although the thought frequented the Apple parents' minds. Verbal warnings and time outs did little to quell the young boy's outbursts. They could strip Barry's room of everything but the sheets and he still seemed to come out worse every time.

18

In the morning, Chloe had dropped the children off at school and was busy kneading dough next to Rebecca at the bakery. Rebecca asked, "Did you ask your husband about having drinks with me sometime?"

Chloe replied, "I mentioned it. He was making jokes, then my son acted out at the table and the evening was ruined. We didn't talk about it again."

Rebecca smiled. She said, "I'm glad I don't have rug rats. I don't think I could handle it."

Chloe said, "I like being a mom. My daughter's really sweet but my son is a tiny terror. It's a little much to handle at times, but I love them both."

"What's their names?"

"Mila and Barry."

Rebecca said, "Beautiful. Barry Apple, huh."

"Yeah, Barry was Peter's grandfather's name."

"That's nice. It sounds like you could use a girl's night out, though. We should make plans."

Chloe's phone began ringing in her pocket. She went to the sink to wash her hands, hoping it wasn't the school. No one usually called her, except Peter, and not normally while he was at work. Chloe prayed it was a solicitation. It stopped ringing by the time she finished washing and she looked at the screen. It was the school. Her stomach turned a couple of backflips when she listened to the voicemail.

It was the principal, asking that she return her call. Chloe pressed the talk button and closed her eyes. She took a deep breath and waited for an answer. The school secretary picked up and put her through to the principal.

When the principal picked up, Chloe braced herself for bad news. The principal said, "Thank you for returning my call quickly. We have an issue with your son."

"Oh my, what's happened?"

"He exhibited poor conduct today. He took another child's lunch box and hit him with it."

"That's horrible." Stress was making Chloe feel sick at this point.

The principal said, "We need you to come to the school to discuss the matter in person, if that's possible."

"Of course. Give me a few minutes to talk to my supervisor and about fifteen to get there."

"Okay, Mrs. Apple. We'll see you when you get here."

Chloe felt embarrassed about having to ask to leave early on her second day back. She told Julissa that Barry had an 'accident' on the playground. All the women stopped what they were doing to express their concerns. Chloe became self-conscious. Her fib already tore at her heart.

Julissa gave her a hug. She said, "Oh, honey, I do hope he's okay."

One of the other women said, "We'll say a prayer. Do you want to say one with us now?"

Chloe replied, "No. I really have to go."

She could feel blood rushing to her face. She knew she must look like a human tomato. She looked at Rebecca, who was the only woman there not chattering and making a fuss. Rebecca stood with a strange look in her hazel eyes. It was a mixture of curiosity and something else Chloe couldn't place. A small smirk let Chloe know that Rebecca saw through her rouse. She could see that Rebecca actually thought the spectacle was amusing.

As Chloe headed for the door, the air seemed to thicken with her lie. Taking a deep breath when she made it outside, Chloe climbed into her car and put the key in the ignition. Her mind was racing. She didn't know what she was going to tell them when she returned. Knowing it was the kind of lie that would haunt her for a while, Chloe wished her friend Rita was still at the bakery. She could always talk to Rita. She wondered if she could confide in Rebecca.

On the way to the school she fought to keep her composure. The thought of Barry being kicked out or suspended on his second day made her want to scream. She hoped that wasn't what she was going to discuss. Refusing to ruin her make-up with tears, she smashed the gas and drove like a maniac to get her mind off the intense frustration she felt.

Chloe fumed over how graduating from 'house-mom' to 'working-mom' could potentially end so quickly. The break from home and the kids was something she needed. It was a necessity, and without it she felt she would explode. She'd barely had one-and-a-half days under her belt now and the thought of losing her new-found freedom infuriated her.

Chloe remembered when Mila had started school. She had been just a little sad to leave her daughter each day; she so enjoyed spending time with her daughter. Now Barry, well, he had his moments. Some of the things he did as he got older were even comical. Overall, he was a handful. She wanted him to be able to attend school and stay out of trouble long enough for her to have a life *away* from him. Feeling a pang of guilt, she increased her speed.

The pressure she was putting on the car proved too much. There was a loud pop and shudder. The dash lit up and smoke began rising from the hood. Chloe cursed and pulled the car to the side of the road. She couldn't believe her luck. Stranded three blocks away from the school, she decided to walk; grabbing her purse, she stepped out of the car and locked it.

Approaching the school, another wave of anxiety washed over her. Questioning herself and biting her lip, she took a deep breath. What's wrong with my little boy? Is it something I've done? How can I change the way he behaves?

The cool air inside the school's hallway made her realize she was sweating. Chloe hastened to a bathroom to freshen up. She didn't usually wear make-up, having been blessed with a natural beauty, and now she cursed herself for deciding to wear cosmetics today.

As Chloe looked into the reflection of her own light blue eyes in the mirror, she wondered how Barry could have such hatred in his eyes. Preparing to face the principal, and feeling like she was the one in trouble, Chloe steadied herself. She hurriedly rummaged through her purse to find her Xanax prescription. Normally she only took it at the end of the day to relax. She felt a twinge of guilt for taking one in the middle of the day to deal with a public confrontation.

Finally arriving at the principal's office Chloe read the sign on the door, 'Administration, Principal Walker'. Her body shuddered as she prepared herself to enter.

19

As soon as Chloe stepped into the interior of the school's administration office, she was greeted by a cheerful receptionist. The lady smiled brightly. She asked, "How can I help you?"

"I'm here about my son, Barry Apple."

"Mrs. Apple! We've been expecting you."

Chloe felt startled by the woman's enthusiasm and energy. The woman continued. "I'm Leeann. Please have a seat." The energetic secretary gestured to some wooden chairs lined against the far wall.

Chloe began surveying her surroundings while she waited. There was a large cork board full of announcements, bulletins for school projects and teachers' events. Chloe busied herself reading some of the documents to keep her mind off the reason she was sitting in the little wooden chair.

The principal's door opened and Mrs. Walker stood in the doorway, in a light green pant suit with a reddish orange blouse. She reminded Chloe of an olive. Realizing she was smirking, because the passive look on the principal's face turned puzzled, Chloe straightened in her chair. The amazon-like woman didn't seem pleased.

Principal Walker said, "It took you quite a while to get here, Mrs. Apple. Is everything okay?"

"I had car trouble a couple of blocks away. I had to walk."

"I suppose that explains it. Come inside my office. We have things of a sensitive nature to discuss."

Chloe stood and followed the principal. Before passing the threshold to the office, she looked over at the hyper-active secretary. The woman was smiling like a lunatic, showing Chloe her fingers were crossed. It made Chloe wonder if she was going to be in some kind of trouble. She felt nervous, like an errant child.

The interior of the principal's office was bland. Everything was clean and organized. The only hangings on the wall were the principal's own achievements. Chloe wondered whether this woman had a family. The principal motioned to a set of black leather upholstered chairs, dotted with finishing studs. They matched the larger chair behind the cherry-wood desk where Principal Walker took a seat. Chloe sat and took a deep breath.

Principal Walker spoke first. She said, "I suppose you're wondering why you're here. Would that be a safe assumption?"

Chloe didn't understand the need for her to state the obvious. Principal Walker's dark green eyes seemed alert and intelligent. Chloe stayed silent, considering it a rhetorical question.

The principal said, "We're here because *Principal Walker* doesn't know what to do with your son today. He attacked another student, and that is not tolerated here at Clinton. Principal Walker will not tolerate his behavior."

Chloe was dumbfounded. She knew Barry had attacked a student, but she was beginning to re-think her initial thought of seeing an intelligence in the principal's eyes: This woman had just referred to herself in third person twice in a row. Chloe was bursting inside, but she didn't let it show. She couldn't stand when people did that.

The principal said, "Do you feed your son at home, Mrs. Apple?"

Chloe was puzzled. She said, "Yes, I feed him."

"Does he get snacks?"

"Not all the time, but yes."

Mrs. Walker made a clucking noise with her mouth. She said, "Barry assaulted his classmate for a pudding snack."

Chloe was speechless. The principal continued, "They were having an outside lunch, and Barry decided he wanted the other boy's treat. He knocked the poor child unconscious. Is Barry an aggressive child at home?"

Chloe thought it would be best to be honest. She said, "Yes, he is. He bites, punches, kicks and scratches. I'm not sure what to do about it. I want him to behave, but everything we try seems to make him worse. How did he knock another student unconscious? He's only five."

"He used the other student's metal lunchbox. Steven Whitaker is the victim's name. He's at the Children's Hospital having his head examined for internal injuries and to deal with his concussion. I suppose you need to try new methods of dealing with your child's aggression. Seek some kind of counseling, outside help. He's in the first grade, public school, not a reformatory. This type of thing will not continue happening on Principal Walker's watch. Principal Walker is not in the business of *anarchy*; there *will* be order. *Period.*"

It was official, this woman made Chloe sick. Barry's actions made her sick, also. She knew there were going to be problems, but she didn't imagine something so severe. Barry had mugged and assaulted another child. She almost didn't want to ask what type of punitive action was going to be taken as a result of the violence he displayed.

Principal Walker asked, "What are the conditions at home, Mrs. Apple?"

Chloe could see exactly where this was heading. She asked, "What do you mean?"

"I'm asking if you and your husband fight. I assume Barry has a father at home, although it wouldn't surprise me, or be unusual, if he didn't."

Turning red in the face, Chloe tried to mask her frustration. It was the psychiatrist conversation all over again. The pompous woman was going to want her to bring Barry to a psychiatrist again. Chloe gritted her teeth. She said, "My Husband and I have arguments, like every couple does, but never in front of the children."

The principal clucked again. She asked, "Where do you suppose he gets these violent tendencies, Mrs. Apple?"

"I'm not sure. It's like he was born with a mean streak."

"I suppose you believe that to be an acceptable excuse. Principal Walker does not." Chloe hooded her eyes. The principal continued, "I haven't seen one of my students be so savagely attacked in all my years. And I've been around quite some time, Mrs. Apple."

In defense, Chloe said, "It couldn't have been that bad."

The principal looked appalled. She said, "I suppose you missed the part where I told you that Barry hospitalized the poor child? It's obvious that the extent of the damage done has yet to sink in. Let's take a look in the incident report folder, where I happen to have a couple of pictures that may change your improper attitude."

Chloe didn't know how to respond, and when the principal pulled out the Polaroids, it only became worse. She felt her mouth dry up and tears threatened the corners of her eyes. Principle Walker had graphic pictures, all of which were heart wrenching. The young boy, Steven Whitaker, was visibly traumatized. His left eye was purple and swollen shut. Then there were pictures of Barry, with his trademark scowl and a chocolate rimmed mouth, the ring of chocolate was evidently from Steven's pudding pack.

Chloe asked, "Where's Barry now?"

Principal Walker sat back in her chair with a smug look on her face. She said, "He's with the school counselor. She's been watching him since the incident. If it were up to me he'd be in juvenile hall."

Chloe's frustration welled up again. She didn't like the principal's remarks. Gaining her composure, she spoke in a restrained tone. She said, "Show me to my son."

"I will. As soon as we talk about the administrative action. Barry will be suspended for three days. He will only be allowed back with a note from a psychiatrist, verifying that he is getting professional help."

Infuriated, Chloe held her tongue, wondering if any other first grade student had been suspended in the history of Clinton Elementary—she didn't want to ask.

20

Walking beside Principal Walker made Chloe feel extra small. She was small, the principal's six feet dwarfed her. The woman got on her nerves, but at the same time, she didn't want to be the one to get into a physical altercation with what she perceived to be the equivalent of a giant. At least a giant compared to other women.

The counselor's office was around the corner, midway down the hall, to the right. Principal Walker opened the door and passed through with Chloe in tow. She smelled the principal's perfume up close for the first time. The sweet and flowery aroma made her dizzy for a fraction of a second. It reminded her of an old lady that used to watch her as a child. The first thing she heard before the principal cleared the doorway was Barry.

He said, "I don't care."

Once in the room, she observed her surroundings. There were small chairs, tables, the usual A, B, C's and 1, 2, 3's that seemed to grace the walls of every child specialist's office. There were stuffed animals in a bin, and the counselor was sitting on the floor with Barry, trying to interact with him. They had toy cars and animals scattered around them. The counselor said, "Barry, you hurt that boy really bad. You must care."

"I don't. You can't make me."

The counselor looked up at Chloe and the principal. She said, "We're not making much progress right now."

Standing, the counselor extended her hand. She was Chloe's age and similar in height and looks. If it wasn't for the counselor's long brown hair and librarian style black frame glasses, she might have been Chloe's double. Chloe took her hand and was shocked at how soft her slim palm was.

The counselor said, "I'm Trisha Taddeo, the school counselor. I'm pleased to make your acquaintance. I presume you're Barry's mother?"

Chloe smiled. She said, "Yes, I'm Chloe Apple."

"Well, it's nice to meet you. You can call me Trisha."

Chloe felt surprised how nice Trisha was. She also felt embarrassed for wanting to ask a personal question. Before she knew it she was asking anyway. It just came spewing out of her mouth as though she were possessed.

"What kind of lotion do you use?"

Trisha paused and looked at Chloe as if analyzing her for a brief moment. The principal interrupted. She asked, "What difference does it make what kind of lotion Counselor Taddeo uses, Mrs. Apple? We're here to talk about your son."

Trisha let go of Chloe's hand. She said, "It's

perfectly fine, Mrs. Walker." She looked Chloe in the eyes. She said, "I use a lot of coco-butter."

Chloe was embarrassed now. She chastised herself internally for asking such an off the subject, personal question, at a time like this.

Barry sat quietly on the floor playing with a fire truck. He didn't even acknowledge the presence of his mother. Trisha said, "I'm very concerned about Barry. He seems to show no remorse for what he's done. I'm afraid that it could be an extremely disturbing sign. I think it would be best if you had a psychiatric evaluation done on him. Either way, the bottom line is, he's going to need special attention. Although it's not abnormal for first graders to fight, it usually isn't this severe, and he has no fear of what's going to happen to him because of his actions, or any other emotion that I can perceive as a direct effect of what he's done."

Chloe didn't know what to say. She knew Barry showed little positive emotion. The whole situation was a waking nightmare. Wanting to be out of the school and on her way home, she began to fidget.

Trisha said, "I have a psychiatrist that I recommend. She's thorough and experienced."

Chloe cringed at the idea. She said, "Sure. What's her name and address?"

Trisha sensed Chloe's reluctance to receive help. She said, "It won't be too bad, Mrs. Apple. Her fees are modest, and she's great with children. Do you know where Kingdom Court drive is?"

Chloe's stomach knotted up and turned a back flip.

She said, "Yes, I know where it is." She knew exactly where it was.

Trisha said, "Perfect. The Doctor's name is Gabriela Payne. She's at 1422 Kingdom Court, suite 609."

Chloe had known it was coming. She had just been referred to the same psychiatrist she had stormed away from a few years prior. She loathed how that event had now turned full circle and was biting her in the backside. Looking down at Barry infuriated her. Why couldn't he be nice?

21

Leaving the school, Chloe felt frustrated and flustered. Barry walked beside her quietly. They crossed the lawn and at the edge of the street, she held out her hand. She said, "Hold my hand while we cross the road."

Barry said, "I don't wanna hold your hand. I'm big enough."

Chloe became furious. She grabbed the loop on his back pack and began crossing. Barry flailed his arms. He said, "Let go."

Chloe didn't say a word. She practically dragged him across the street. He plopped down on the curb on the other side. The look on his face, murderous.

Chloe said, "You better get up and follow me. We have to walk, and I've got to make a phone call. I've already had enough of your nonsense. After today you'll be lucky if your father and I don't take all your toys and television until you straighten up, mister. You're definitely not getting any snacks in the near future. So sit there and make it worse, or come with me."

He stood and began following her. Chloe fished her

phone out of her pocket, while making distance from the school with Barry on her heels. The thought of other parents showing up gave her goosebumps. She felt sick inside, thinking that soon everyone would know what he'd done. There would be endless questions and judgmental looks from other school parents, and probably from her co-workers as well.

Chloe called the person she always called in emergencies: Her hero, Peter. She hated to call him at work, but she had waited as long as she could. Needing to hear his voice, wanting him to solve all her problems, she pressed her cheek to the phone, which seemed to ring for an eternity. At last, Peter answered, and at just the sound of his voice she felt herself relax the slightest bit.

She spoke with an urgency in her tone. She said, "I have a problem."

Peter said, "Calm down, sugar plum. You know there's no such thing. '*WE have a problem*,' is the phrase. Now, tell me what's going on."

"Well, honey—I had to come to the school because Barry is in trouble and the car broke down."

"Okay, sugar. Do I need to go to the school?"

"No, I picked Barry up. He's right…" Chloe looked down, Barry was nowhere near her. She looked up the street in the direction she'd come and spotted him sitting on the sidewalk. He was staring at her.

She said, "That little brat. He stopped following me. He's sitting up the street with a defiant look on his face. Oohh… I could really kick his little butt right now."

Peter said, "Now, Chloe. Don't do anything rash. Wait a few minutes and go back for him. Do you want me to come pick you up?"

Chloe turned her back on Barry. She couldn't stand the sight of him at the moment. Her insides felt like they were boiling. Feeling beads of sweat collect on her forehead, and tears threatening the corners of her eyes, she wanted to scream.

She said, "I would like to get as far away from the school as possible. I don't want to be on this street when parents start showing up."

Peter said, "Sugar, parents won't start arriving for another thirty or forty minutes. I could pick you two up and we could get Mila. I'll deal with the car later. What street are you on?"

Chloe huffed and bit her lip. She said, "I'm on Clarice Street. But hurry up. I'm serious, mister."

"Just stay calm, sugar. I'm on my way."

Chloe disconnected and turned around to check on Barry. Her heart skipped a beat. Mouth went dry. Hands became numb. He was gone.

22

Running to where Barry had been sitting, Chloe spun in a circle, looking. She felt panicked and dizzy. A sickness welled in her stomach. He had vanished.

She began yelling, "Barry! Barry where are you!"

Tears spilled from her eyes and ran down her cheeks. She was still holding her phone, so she lifted it to dial. Her hands were shaking so badly that she could barely manage calling Peter back.

By the time Peter answered, Chloe was hysterical. She sobbed into the phone, unable to get a word out. Peter asked, "What's the matter? Are you hurt?" His voice was tinged with alarm.

Chloe shuddered and stuttered. She said, "H-h-he's g-gone, Peter. I don't know w-where he's at."

"Barry's gone? Do you think someone took him? I thought you were watching him."

"I w-was, but I got so mad that I t-turned around. N-now he's gone."

Sitting quietly for a moment, Peter listened to Chloe sob. He said, "Stay exactly where you are, call the police. I'm on my way. I'll be there as fast I can possibly get there. Try to calm down, baby. Do what has to be done, okay?"

"Okay, but hurry. I'm so scared. I can barely s-stand."

"I'm on my way. We have to hang up, and you have to call the police, right now."

"Okay, Peter. I love you. Please don't be mad at me."

"I'm not mad, sugar. We have to think of Barry right now."

Chloe hung up with Peter and dialed 911. A lady answered.

"Nine-one-one, what's your emergency?"

Chloe was nervous and upset; she felt faint. She said, "My son is missing."

"How old is your son, ma'am?"

"He's five."

"Where did he go missing from?"

"We were on the sidewalk by his school and now he's gone."

"Could you give me your location?"

"Yes."

Chloe looked at the address of the house she was standing in front of. She said, "I'm at 2001 Clarice Street. I'm standing in front of the house he was sitting at when he went missing."

"What's your name?"

"Chloe Apple."

"What's your son's name?"

"Barry Apple"

"Okay, ma'am. I'm dispatching a unit your way now. Stay calm and stay put."

"I will. I'm not going anywhere."

The operator said, "We can stay on the line, if you don't mind."

"I don't mind. I'll stay on the line."

Chloe could hear sirens in the distance. They were close and getting closer. The operator asked, "Were you picking him up early?"

Chloe became apprehensive. She said, "Yes."

"A unit should arrive shortly. You're doing fine."

The sirens were close now. Then they went silent and Chloe saw two blue and white squad cars turn on the street. Their lights were still lit, and they were traveling fast. Her heart felt like it might explode.

Chloe said, "They're here."

"Okay, ma'am. Is there anything else you need before we disconnect?"

"No, thank you."

23

Police cars came to a screeching halt in front of the residence. It took all the strength Chloe could muster just to not pass out. She felt the heat coming from the police cruiser. The officers exited their vehicles. They were an odd pair.

One stood short, almost Chloe's height, he was stocky, like a steroid junky. He had large eyes that seemed to protrude from their sockets. His bald head shined in the sunlight. Skin the color of coal.

The other stood over six feet tall and skinny. He wore a crew cut, his eyes were beady and close together. He had large ears that were an alarming contrast to his eyes. Skin disturbingly pale, like he rarely went out in the daytime.

They approached Chloe and she read their name tags. The short one's tag read Dixon and the tall one's read Tinsel. Officer Dixon asked, "Did you place a call about a missing child?"

Chloe tried to stay calm. She said, "Yes. I'm Chloe Apple, my son Barry is missing."

Officer Tinsel asked, "Can you tell us exactly what

happened, ma'am?"

Officer Tinsel's deep voice was strange to Chloe, she thought it sounded like he was doing it intentionally. Trying not to focus on things of a frivolous nature, she began to explain her situation. She said, "I broke down a couple of blocks away and he quit following me. I took my eyes off of him for just a few seconds and he's gone." Chloe began to tear up.

Officer Dixon said, "Try to stay calm, ma'am. The situation is going to be under control. Have any vehicles passed since you've been on this street?"

Chloe thought. She said, "No. I don't remember any."

Officer Tinsel asked, "Do you think there's a chance that he went back to the school?"

Chloe was uncertain. She said, "I guess he could have."

Officer Dixon asked, "Did you see anyone suspicious while you were walking?"

Chloe thought about the question. She began fidgeting. She said, "I don't remember seeing anyone. I was arguing with Barry and then I was talking on the phone. I wasn't paying attention."

Officer Tinsel asked, "How would you describe your son? What was he wearing?"

"He has blonde hair and blue eyes. He's five and comes up to my thigh. He was wearing dark blue overalls and had on a red short-sleeve shirt."

Officer Tinsel asked, "Is there anything else you can tell me? I'm going to radio in with his description, anything you can think of could be useful."

Chloe concentrated. She said, "He has an Incredible Hulk back pack and he's missing his front teeth, on the top."

Officer tinsel went to his car to radio in. Officer Dixon stood with Chloe and propped his short log-like arms so that one was under his chest and the other's elbow was in its palm. Putting his hand to his mouth he raised his eyebrows. He seemed to be studying Chloe for a minute.

He said, "He probably wandered off on his own. I'm hoping that when we canvas the neighborhood and school we'll find him. It's a terrible thing when a child goes missing. I can't imagine what you're going through."

Chloe said, "This is a living nightmare. My nerves are shot. I'm so worried."

"You're doing well, Mrs. Apple. I'm sure the situation will be resolved shortly."

Peter's truck screeched around the corner, drawing officer Dixon and Chloe's attention. He sped up the street and came to a quick halt behind officer Tinsel's cruiser. Before he opened his door Chloe ran for the truck. He stepped out and she flung herself in his arms, unable to hold her hysteria within any longer. Peter held her tight and whispered reassurances in her ear while she sobbed.

24

The streets were crawling with police. When school let out, it became obvious that Barry was going to be much harder to find. Chloe and Peter were on the school grounds with Mila. The principal, school counselor and several teachers were huddled around the Apple family. Everyone was expressing their concern.

Principal Walker said, "I'm absolutely disturbed. It would be some kind of bold individual who would snatch a child up with his mother just feet away."

A news crew arrived and approached the group. Principal Walker stepped out and confronted them. She said, "I don't suppose the family wants to be plastered on channel six news right now."

Chloe said, "It's okay, Principal Walker. I'll talk to them."

The reporter had a glowing smile. She said, "I'm Latisha Lenox. Can you tell me what happened here today?" Her smile was disturbing to Chloe. She didn't know how anyone could be asking about a missing child with a smile on their face. She wondered if the woman was high on something.

After the interview, there was an uproar. A police officer walked up to the crowd with Barry. Relief washed over Chloe and she began to feel faint again. The stress leaving her body was almost as taxing as being in the heightened state of panic she was in when the situation began. Officer Tinsel delivered Barry to Peter and Chloe with a concerned look in his beady eyes.

He said, "Here's your boy, Mr. and Misses Apple." His voice was still oddly deep and unwavering, but something in his tone suggested Barry had been up to no good.

Barry had his trademark scowl on and wouldn't look at anyone. The reporter asked, "Can we get a comment?"

Officer Tinsel said, "I'd like to address the parents first." He turned to Peter and Chloe. He said, "The homeowner of the residence where you made the report from came home and found your son inside. He made a mess and there are some damages. I'm not sure how to file the report on a five-year-old. I'm pretty sure the parents are liable in a situation like this. He broke some lamps and threw everything in the refrigerator on the floors."

Peter looked at Barry. He said, "What were you thinking, son?"

Barry stared at the ground with his brow knit. Officer Tinsel said, "It's also apparent he defecated on the living room carpet and may have urinated on the couches."

The reporter stood with her microphone and camera man close. Her incredulous smile never leaving her face. She asked, "Mr. Apple, can I get a comment for the evening news?"

Peter confronted the reporter. He said, "We're just happy Barry is safe and back with us. He has some issues we'll be seeking help for, but the important thing is that he's okay."

25

In the truck, everyone was silent. Chloe was fuming. Peter sat in deep thought, staring at Chloe's broken down Toyota. Shaking his head, he released a grunt.

He said, "I think we'll call a tow truck. I don't think I feel like being on the side of the road fixing a car right now."

He wrote down the address of the house and called a local wrecker. They sat and waited for the service provider to arrive. After a long and uncomfortable silence, Peter turned the radio on. Chloe leaned forward and turned it back off. She stared at Peter. Ignoring her for a minute, he took a deep breath.

He asked, "What is it, sugar plum?"

Chloe said, "You need to talk to your son." In a calm voice that sent shivers up his spine.

Peter turned in his seat to face Barry. He asked, "What happened today, buddy?"

Barry said, "I just wanted the puddin'."

Peter looked at Chloe. He said, "He wanted pudding."

Chloe slapped Peter on the arm. She said, "He's a

deviant. We have to do something or it's going to get worse."

"Sugar, we can't do much on the side of the road. Let's try to relax for a minute and think of solutions."

Chloe let a frustrated groan escape her lips. She leaned forward and turned the radio on. The family sat without speaking a word until the tow truck arrived. When it arrived, Barry lit up. It was one of those rare occasions when he actually smiled. He was in awe of the large red truck with flat bed. Peter exited the vehicle with Barry and went to talk to the driver. Chloe turned the radio's volume low and turned in her seat. She could see tear streaks on Mila's cheeks.

Chloe asked, "Are you okay, sweetie?"

Mila shuddered. She said, "I don't want to go back to school."

Chloe's heart ached for her little girl. She said, "Don't worry, baby. Everything's going to be okay. You'll see."

Mila wiped her eyes with the sleeves of her shirt. She said, "Everybody seen. They're all gonna make fun of me. Veronica and Sandra won't even want to be my friends no more."

"Sweetie. I'm sure they're going to be your friends. Why wouldn't they be?"

"I was watching everyone, Mommy. They're all gonna be mean. I know it."

26

At home the family sat down for dinner. Chloe served leftover meatloaf and green beans. Everyone ate in silence. Peter finished his plate and watched the family. Mila took small bites. It wasn't hard to see that she was somber. Barry had food all over himself and the table.

When Chloe finished, she began picking up plates. She asked, "Who wants dessert?"

Mila sank down in her seat. Peter said, "I'll have some."

Chloe smiled. "Good. Apple pie and ice cream for you and Mila."

Barry said. "I want ice cream."

Chloe replied, "That's too bad, Barry Apple. After the stunts you pulled today, you're lucky we don't send you away."

Barry knocked his plate to the ground and stormed to his room. Chloe said, "Peter. Do something."

"You're provoking him at the table. You had to know something like that was going to happen."

"That's beside the point, babe. We have to start

doing something now. He's getting worse and worse. Please, punish him."

"Are you suggesting I spank him? You were always the one so vehemently against physical punishment. Really, I'm not much for that myself. You know the kinds of beatings I took as a child."

"We can't just let him get away with all this crap, Peter. We have to do something."

"What do you suggest?"

Chloe turned red in the face. She said, "Go in there and take away everything. Forbid him to come out of that room."

27

Peter went to the hall closet and pulled out moving boxes. He went to Barry's room and started packing everything in sight. Chloe joined him. Barry sat on the bed quietly, with a grim look on his face. They spent a couple of hours collecting and cleaning until the room was bare of everything except clothes, bed and basics.

They put all the boxes in the garage and Chloe gave Peter a hug. She asked, "What are we going to do, babe?"

Peter said, "Whatever it takes, sugar plum. We'll get him straightened out."

"What if nothing works, Peter? What if he turns out even worse?"

"He'll turn out just fine, sugar."

"They said I have to get professional help for him. They referred me to Dr. Payne."

"I'm sure the psychiatrist isn't holding a grudge against you. It'll be fine."

Chloe sighed, she felt chaotic inside. She said, "I have to get the kids ready for bed."

"Do you want help?"

"No. I know you want to get cleaned up. Take a shower and I'll meet you in the room when I have them settled in."

"I'll tell you what, sugar plum. You get them ready and when I get out of the shower I'll have a talk with them both."

Chloe smiled. She said, "That's a good idea."

Peter went to shower and Chloe helped Mila get ready for bed first. Mila was somber and Chloe could see that the day's events were still weighing heavily on her. Her heart went out to the poor girl. Worry marked Mila's features.

Chloe asked, "Do you want to talk about school some more?"

Mila shuddered. She said, "I don't want to think about it, Mommy. I just want to lay down."

Chloe left Mila's room feeling disturbed. She knew her little girl was going through something she couldn't fix. She only hoped that the kids at school wouldn't be cruel. Anxiety overwhelmed her when she thought of Mila being tormented.

Chloe visited Barry's room next. He was sitting with his legs crossed on the bed. His face was screwed into an angry expression. Chloe wondered if he had been sitting with the same expression the whole time she'd been gone, or if he put it on when he heard her coming in. It didn't matter much either way, she thought, he always seemed to be aggravated.

She said, "It's time to get ready for bed."

Barry sat still and quiet. Chloe asked, "Are you going

to cooperate?"

"No." His concise reply.

"Your dad's going to be in here in a minute. Do you want me to tell him you're being uncooperative?"

"I don't care."

Chloe left Barry's room frustrated and found Peter in their bedroom getting into his night pants and t-shirt. She sat on the bed and released an exasperated sigh. Peter asked, "What's wrong, sugar?"

Chloe flopped back with her arms out to both sides. She said, "YOUR son is a little devil."

Peter chuckled. He said, "My son, huh? Last I checked you birthed him. How do I know he's not the milk man's?"

Chloe growled and snatched a pillow, flinging it at him. She giggled. She said, "You're not funny. You need to go do something about him. He's out of control."

"Believe me, sugar. I get it. With everything he does and all the people I have to hear it from, I know. There's not much we can do that we don't do already. I'll talk to him and we'll get help. Unless you have other suggestions."

Chloe rolled her eyes and flopped back into the bed again. She said, "I just want him to behave. I want him to be normal."

Peter laughed. He said, "Behave, maybe, but I don't think OUR little oddball is going to be normal anytime soon."

Chloe sat up. She said, "You're so bad. Please, go

talk to him. He's getting on my last nerve."

"I'm going, I'm going. Just relax, have a drink or something."

"Should I call Rebecca?"

"Who's Rebecca?"

Chloe smirked and cocked her head to the side. Peter contained his laughter. He said, "Wait until the weekend, sugar. That would be a better time for you and your work girlfriend to go out and kiss on each other."

Chloe groaned and rolled her eyes. She said, "I can't believe you. Why do you insist on making things weird?"

"You know I'm just playing, sugar plum. Is she hot?"

Chloe giggled. "I'm going to punch you, mister. I'm talking knuckle sandwiches."

Peter wanted to double over with laughter. Chloe picked up another pillow and threw it. She missed. Peter said, "I like it when you're mad."

Chloe balled her fist and shook it in front of her. She said, "I'm not mad yet, buddy boy. Go talk to your son. Don't think you're getting lucky when you come back, either."

"Yes, ma'am. I'm movin'. We'll see about that last part when I get back."

Chloe smiled and shook her head. "You're the worst. You really are."

"Thank you, baby. It means a lot."

Peter turned to walk out and mooned her leaving the

threshold of the room. Chloe giggled and flopped back on the bed to watch the ceiling fan. She loved how Peter could turn her sour mood into a good one. Hoping he could get through to Barry, she closed her eyes to pray

28

Peter stepped into Barry's room and found him fully clothed sitting in the small wooden chair in the corner. He had his shoes on the wrong feet and was trying to tie them. He didn't even look up from what he was doing to see who had walked in. The room was dark except for the night light, so Peter pulled the cord on Barry's ceiling fan and shed some light on his comical looking son.

Peter asked, "What are you doing, buddy? Are you going somewhere?"

Barry kept his head down and concentrated on tying knots. He said, "I'm going for a walk. I'm mad."

"It's too late to walk, bubba. I'm ready for bed and you can't go alone."

Barry looked up with a scowl. He said, "I don't wanna be here."

Peter replied, "It isn't negotiable, son. You're not going anywhere. Why don't you take off your shoes and sit over here on the bed with me?" Peter crossed the room and sat on Barry's super hero clad mattress.

Barry kicked his shoes off and went to sit next to his

father. Peter ran his fingers through Barry's hair. He said, "It's about time for a haircut. How about we go do that this weekend? How's that sound?"

Barry said, "I like the haircut lady."

Peter laughed. He said, "I know you do. She gives you suckers if you sit still, doesn't she?"

Barry grinned. He said, "Yeah. I like her."

Peter cleared his throat and pulled Barry close to his side. He said, "Why have you been giving your mother such a hard time?"

"She's always tellin' me what to do."

"She's your mother, buddy. She's supposed to tell you what to do. You shouldn't push her away so much."

They sat quietly for a moment. There was a lot to talk about but Peter wanted to take his time. He wanted Barry to talk to him, to confide in him. Peter knew forcing him to explain himself would be a disaster. He understood how to deal with Barry a little better than Chloe did. Not that Chloe was a bad mother, she just hadn't dealt with many belligerent hard-heads, other than Peter himself. Peter had been a rambunctious young boy and he understood more about Barry and his behavior.

Peter asked, "Do you want to talk about your day? Maybe tell me what happened at school? It helps to talk about these kinds of things. I know how it feels to be in trouble."

Barry said, "I wanted a puddin'."

"Yeah you told me that part, bud. Why did you hit

that boy with the lunch box?"

"I took the puddin' and he tried to take it back."

Peter ran his fingers through his own hair. He said, "Son, it just isn't right to take things from people by force."

"I asked him, Poppa. He wouldn't give it to me."

"It was his pudding, Barry. You took something that wasn't yours and then hurt him when he wanted it back. Can you see how that's wrong?"

"I guess."

Peter was exasperated but tried not to let it show. The conversation and the way Barry behaved ninety percent of the time was a lot to bear. Always trying to keep his cool, he'd had plenty of talks with Barry in the past. He couldn't see any benefit in corporal punishment at this stage and he didn't know if he would even be capable of inflicting pain on his son as punishment. He had to try to get through to him.

Peter said, "You make things bad for yourself and all of us when you do things like you did today. There were a lot of people worried about you when you disappeared. Do you realize how you made everyone feel?"

"No."

"Well, it's bad. Probably the worst thing of all, but it's all bad. We have to pay for the damages to the people's house you broke in to. Why did you do that?"

"Momma said I couldn't have any snacks or toys when I got home and I wanted to play. So I went in the house and ate snacks and played with toys."

Peter felt ashamed. He said, "Son, you peed and pooped on their furniture and floors."

"I had to go."

"Why didn't you use their bathroom?"

"Their bathroom was nasty."

As singular and ridiculous as it sounded, Barry's response brought a minute amount of relief to Peter. He was glad that it wasn't just a malicious act. Even though the situation was no less extreme, knowing that his son wasn't a complete deviant helped. He took a deep breath and patted Barry on the back.

Peter said, "We can talk some more tomorrow. It's time to get ready for bed. It's too late for a bath, but I'll get your jammies. Get out of those dirty clothes and we'll get you changed and tucked in. How does that sound?"

Barry yawned and rubbed his eyes. He said, "Okay, Poppa."

Peter tucked him in. He asked, "Do you want your door closed all the way?"

Barry replied, "No. I want the hall light, and could you close the closet?"

Peter closed the closet door and turned the ceiling fan light off. When he exited the room, he left the bedroom door ajar and walked away with a smile. His son was no monster; he was still just a little boy underneath it all. Peter wished the rest of the world could see Barry the way he did.

29

When Peter entered his bedroom Chloe was in their master bathroom showering. He kicked off his slippers and laid in the bed. He heard the shower turn off and Chloe poked her head out the door. Peter always loved the way she looked with wet hair.

She asked, "How did it go? Is the little heathen in bed?"

"Yeah, sugar, he's laying down."

"How did your talk go?"

"I'd say it went well. I think he's going to come around, but it's hard to tell. You know how he is with me compared to anyone else."

Chloe huffed. She said, "I can't believe how rotten he is."

Peter laughed. He said, "Imagine that. A rotten Apple."

Chloe rolled her eyes and disappeared behind the bathroom door again. Peter turned on the television and found the evening news. Chloe was running the hair dryer and he could barely hear, but he didn't want to turn it up. Latisha Lenox was on, a recap of the earlier news broadcast. She was covering the disappearance of Barry. Then it cut to live news and the anchor for the evening news was saying how the faculty of Clinton elementary and parents were outraged. Peter shut the television off in fear that Chloe would look out or hear.

When she came out she was in a sheer nightgown that made it easy to see she was bare underneath. Peter said, "I thought I wasn't getting lucky."

Chloe showed a sly grin. She said, "I've changed my mind."

Crossing the room, she climbed in bed. She started to pull Peter's t-shirt off. He was conflicted whether he should tell her about the news broadcast, knowing she had a pretty good idea about what people were going to say. Chloe pulled his t-shirt over his head and flung it over the side of the bed and began kissing him. Leaning in, he reciprocated. They embraced each other tight, and Peter let go of his worries and became one with his wife.

30

Chloe woke and looked at the bedside alarm clock. Her vision blurred; she rubbed her eyes and looked again. It was 3:04 in the morning. She wasn't sure what woke her. Feeling like she was being watched, she looked around the dark room. There was a small figure at the end of her bed. Her skin crawled.

She asked, "Barry, is that you?"

Barry stood silent and she couldn't see his eyes, but she knew he was watching her. She asked, "Is there something wrong?"

Barry said, "I had a bad dream. I want to sleep with you and dad."

It was an odd request. Barry hadn't ever asked to sleep with them. Chloe pulled the covers back. She said, "Come on, sweetie. Climb up."

Barry went to the bedside and climbed up and over Chloe to rest in-between his parents. Chloe pulled him close and was surprised he didn't push her away. They lay silent for a moment, Chloe held Barry tight. He was shivering. Chloe asked, "Do you want to talk about your dream?"

Barry lay shivering in his mother's arms and didn't make a peep. Chloe wondered what kind of dream could have him so shook up. She said, "We can talk about it in the morning if you want, baby."

She kissed him on top of his head and closed her eyes. Barry said, "The house was on fire and I couldn't find Mila."

Chloe opened her eyes. She said, "That's sounds horrible, sweetie. It wasn't real though."

Barry said, "It seemed real. I was hot and smoke was choking me. Mila was somewhere screaming but I couldn't find her."

Chloe ran her fingers through Barry's hair, realizing he had been sweating. She said, "You're safe. Both of you are safe."

Barry said, "I think I started the fire."

Chloe wasn't sure what to say. She listened to Barry and Peter breath. She wondered if Barry had ever played with fire, besides when the family would go camping, when they let him light his own sparkler from the campfire. It worried her to think that he might actually burn the house down while they slept. She searched for the words that would detour him from that path. Something that would make him feel better and make him against setting a fire. She opened her mouth to speak, but Barry spoke first.

He said, "I don't like fire. I don't want to be bad no more, Momma. I want to be good."

Chloe squeezed Barry tight. She said, "It's okay, baby. You can be good if you want. Let's get some sleep, mommy's tired."

31

The next morning Chloe helped Mila get ready for school and sent her with Peter, since her car was inoperable. She sat down in the living room with Barry and called the bakery. Anxious, she felt tempted to hang up without talking to anyone. Imagining what it was going to be like when she returned made her stomach queasy.

Rebecca answered, "Puff's Bakery, how can I help you?"

Chloe recognized Rebecca's voice. She said, "Rebecca, can I talk to Julissa?"

Rebecca said, "What's going on, momma? Is everything okay?"

Chloe could hear concern in Rebecca's voice. She didn't want to have an in-depth conversation about her troubles over the phone. She said, "Everything's going to be fine. I just need to talk to Julissa."

"Hold on, I'll get her for you."

Chloe sat on hold for a couple of minutes, then Julissa picked up. "Hello, Chloe?"

Chloe's anxiety was through the roof. She hoped she

wouldn't have to explain herself too much. She said, "I need the rest of the week off."

Julissa said, "Oh no, is there anything I can help you with?"

Chloe said, "No. I just have some things I have to take care of and I won't be able to come in. I'll be back next week."

Julissa said, "No worries, dear. You take as much time as you need. We'll be praying for you here, honey."

"Thanks, Julissa. I really appreciate it. It's absurd that I'm calling in so soon."

"Nonsense, dear."

"I'm glad you're so understanding, Julissa."

"Of course, honey. You just call me on my cell Sunday evening if you're not going to be in on Monday."

"I will."

Chloe disconnected with Julissa and her hands were shaking. She wasn't sure how she was going to face the women at the bakery. Tempted to quit the job, she knew if she did, she would regret it. It would be hard to find somewhere that was as lenient as Puff's. Overall, the women there seemed to care about one another and had treated Chloe nicely. She put the phone down and laid on the couch. Barry walked up and sat down in front of her.

He asked, "Can we go for a walk, Momma?"

"It's too early, sweetie. Mommy wants to rest."

Barry said, "Okay." Then he climbed onto the couch

with Chloe.

Chloe was surprised. No trademark scowl. No fit throwing. She thought that the dream must have really scared him. Maybe even enough to change him. Wondering how long his good behavior would last, she pulled him close for a hug.

32

Mila knew she was going to have a rough day at school. Peter pulled to the curb of the Clinton elementary grounds and put the truck in park. He looked over at Mila and she could feel him watching her, waiting for her to turn her head and speak. She didn't want to look at him. She didn't want to look out the window at the kids on the school yard. Staring at the dash she wished she didn't have to get out. Wishing she never had to come back and face the kids or teachers, she felt embarrassed. She hadn't even been approached yet, but she already wanted to cry.

Peter said, "How're you feeling, munchkin?"

She felt afraid to speak. Wanting to plead with her father. Everything in her wanted to protest once again how much she didn't want to go to school. She couldn't fathom how her parents didn't understand her anguish.

Peter said, "You know you wouldn't be able to run forever. No use trying."

She turned to face her father. Peter said, "That's what I want to see. Those baby blue eyes. You know you're too strong to let a little embarrassment hold you back. I bet it isn't going to be half as bad as you imagine."

Mila wished she was as confident as her father. Wondering if he'd ever felt like she did right now, she fought back tears. He looked handsome and strong. His green eyes fixed and unwavering—she wondered how he did it? How could he convey so much in his eyes? He didn't seem to fear anything.

Mila said, "I just wish I could take a day off. It just happened yesterday and everyone's going to want to talk to me."

Peter said, "Imagine that. Like a celebrity. I can see it now. They'll probably want autographs."

Mila smiled. She loved her father's goofy sense of humor. She said, "It's nothing like a celebrity, Dad." She giggled and smiled from ear to ear. "There's no cameras."

"Well, cameras are annoying anyway. That's why so many famous people get in trouble for beating up camera men."

Mila laughed again. She said, "I'm not beating anyone up."

"Nah, I don't suppose so. You're too sweet for all that. You want to run up to the hardware? I'll get some red carpet and roll it out so you can make an entrance."

Her laughter became uncontrollable. She put her hand on her father's arm. She said, "No, no, no. Please, Daddy. I'm gonna die."

"Don't do that, baby girl. All your fans are gonna miss you if you do that."

"I've got to go, Dad. I'm gonna be late."

"That's the spirit, munchkin. Get in there and give 'em hell."

"Oooh... you cursed."

Peter winked. He said, "Don't tell your momma." He put his pinky out and Mila wrapped hers around his and rolled her eyes. "I won't."

Climbing out of the truck smiling, she felt confident. She loved her dad. He always knew how to make her feel better. Ready to face the day, she headed inside the school.

33

Chloe woke and felt around behind herself. Barry wasn't there. Panic rose from her stomach to her chest when she looked around the room and he couldn't be found. Going from room to room she couldn't find him in the house. She called his name—no reply. Approaching the back door, she looked out the pane glass window into the yard and spotted him sitting beneath the tree in the back of the yard. Breathing deeply, she calmed down instead of storming outside in frustration.

Gathering her composure, she walked into the back yard almost all the way up to Barry before he took notice. The look in his eyes—distant and dull—was disconcerting. Though Chloe was happy he hadn't run off again, she worried what Barry might be thinking. His eyes cleared by the time she reached him. He looked upset.

Chloe asked, "Is everything okay, sweetie? What are you doing out here?"

"I just wanted to feel the wind. I've been thinking."

"What are you thinking?"

"I want a puppy."

"Sweetie, you know how your father feels about animals. Especially dogs."

"He won't be that much trouble. I'll take care of him."

"Honey, a dog is a lot of work. They make all kinds of messes and dig holes in the yard. You can't stop one from doing all those things."

"I bet if you talk to poppa he'll let me have one. I'll be good and I'll take care of him. I promise."

Chloe sighed and sat down next to Barry. She asked, "Why do you want a puppy so badly?"

Barry looked at the ground. He said, "The bad man scares me. If I get a puppy and he gets big he can protect me."

Chloe felt startled and alarmed. She visually searched the fence line and looked up in the tree. She had goose bumps. She asked, "What bad man? Where is he?"

Barry said, "He's just in my dreams, but I know he's real. One day he's going to come get me and I need a dog to protect me. The dog would be my best friend. He won't let the man with yellow eyes take me away."

The panic Chloe felt ebbed. She was relieved to find out he was talking about someone in a dream, but she also felt concerned. She said, "Sweetie, you never complained of bad dreams before. Did you see something on television that might be causing all of this?"

"I don't know, Momma. I don't think so. It just started happening. I want it to go away. I'll be good. I promise."

Chloe pulled Barry close and he didn't pull away. He trembled in her arms. The dreams he'd been having were shaking him to the core. It concerned Chloe deeply. She wanted him to be good, but she didn't want him to be tormented.

She said, "Let's go inside, honey. I'll make you something to eat and then mommy has to make a phone call."

They walked inside hand in hand. Barry said, "I'm sorry I'm so mean. I couldn't help it. I know I should be good."

Chloe said, "Don't worry, sweetie. Mommy's going to get help. Everything is going to be okay."

When they entered the house, Chloe locked the door. She said, "You go sit at the table and I'm going to fix you a sandwich. Do you want peanut butter or do you want tuna?"

"Tuna."

"Okay, sit tight."

Chloe made Barry his sandwich and placed it in front of him with potato chips and a glass of grape juice. She went back to the kitchen counter and stared at the phone for a minute. She didn't want to have to call Dr. Payne. She didn't want to admit she was wrong and make amends. Picking up the phone, she walked to the fridge where the phone number hung on a magnet. Shucking her pride, she dialed the number.

34

Dr. Payne's secretary answered, Chloe paused before speaking. The secretary asked, "Is anyone there? Hello?"

Chloe snapped out of it. She said, "Yes, I'd like to make an appointment."

"Okay. Can I have your name?"

"My name is Chloe Apple, and I'm making an appointment for my son, Barry."

"Okay. Have you visited us before?"

"Yes, a couple of years ago."

"Oh, I remember you now."

"Yes, well, I need to see the doctor by the end of the week."

"Okay. I see. It doesn't look like we have any openings until next Tuesday. That's one week."

Chloe rolled her eyes. She didn't let herself get frustrated, or give up just because she would rather not see Gabriela Payne. She took a deep breath, and said, "My son had some trouble at school and he has to see a therapist before he can return. I'm sure you can appreciate my predicament. The school counselor,

Trisha Taddeo, suggested we visit Dr. Payne."

The secretary said, "Okay. One moment please."

She put Chloe on hold for several minutes. Wondering if the woman wanted her to hang up, Chloe rolled her eyes. Returning to the line, the secretary cleared her throat. "Mrs. Apple?"

"Yes."

"Dr. Payne managed an appointment for Friday at twelve o'clock. She's going to see you on her lunch break. Be prompt because she doesn't normally do this."

"I'll be there. Thank you."

"Certainly. Take care."

Chloe hung the phone up and wondered if Dr. Payne was going to be cordial. Hoping that she wasn't making a mistake going to her, she tried not to think negatively. Wanting Barry back in school and herself back at work, she'd do what it takes. Maybe the doctor could help him, or it could all go very badly. She looked over at Barry eating his sandwich and chips and shook her head. The troubles she endured behind him were sure to end one day. She prayed it would before something even more drastic happened.

35

At school, Mila wasn't having as difficult a time as she'd anticipated. Veronica and Sandra were still talking to her and only a handful of students had approached her about Barry. Most of them were curious about when he would be back. A couple thought the whole thing was hilarious. She knew the adults didn't think it was hilarious at all. She was once again becoming wallpaper to the crowd, the way she liked it. Not that she didn't enjoy positive attention, she just couldn't stand negative attention, and she didn't think Barry's antics were funny.

One boy concerned her most—a big kid she had seen around. His curly red hair and freckles were alarming to Mila, reminding her of a crazed carnival clown. She didn't want to ask his name, because she didn't want any rumors or harassment about her showing any interest in him. She'd witnessed it happen too many times to other girls, and she wanted to avoid that kind of attention.

This boy approached Mila and said, "You're that kid's sister. The one who sent the other boy to the hospital." Mila shuffled her feet uncomfortably.

Mila said, "*I* didn't send anyone to the hospital."

The boy laughed, an evil, bone-grinding sound. He said, "You're lucky you're cute or I'd kick your ass."

The boy walked away leaving Mila reeling with shock. She'd never tell anyone about the confrontation. The sinister boy scared her. Not wanting anything to do with him, she hoped he never spoke to her again. Walking to class, she trembled inside. He had threatened her and she didn't even know his name. He was older. Thinking he was probably a fifth grader, she resolved to be on the lookout for him and avoid him as best she could.

The rest of the day went by without complication and she didn't see the boy again. When her father picked her up, she climbed in the truck and buckled her seat belt. He asked, "How was your day, munchkin?"

Mila said, "It was okay."

They began to pull away and Mila looked into the crowd of kids outside her window, onto the school lawn. She almost lost her breath when she spotted the red-headed boy by the school building, looking directly at her. She hoped the boy would just lose interest, praying he would quit looking at her with his beady green eyes—that he would just leave her alone.

As Peter pulled away from the school onto the street, Mila felt relieved. She hadn't had a boy look at her like that boy did. Knowing he might end up being a problem, she tried to rid her mind of foul thoughts. She leaned back in her seat, glad the day was over.

Peter asked, "How were the kids? Did anyone give you trouble?"

"No. Not really."

"Not really? Did something happen? You sound troubled."

"There was this one boy."

"What about him?"

"I just think he's going to be trouble."

"What makes you say that?"

"I don't know. He just seems like trouble. He has a weird laugh."

"You can tell he's going to be trouble by the way he laughs."

"Daddy, you can tell all kinds of things about people in all kinds of ways. You told me that."

"That's right, munchkin. I did, didn't I? Well, if you think he's going to be trouble, you should steer clear."

"Oh, I will. I don't want anything to do with him. I think he likes me in some kind of weird way though."

"A lot of boys are gonna like you, baby girl. You're pretty. Plus, you're a celebrity now. Remember?"

Mila laughed and rolled her eyes. "Stop playing, Dad. Barry's the celebrity."

"He's rotten is what he is." Peter smiled.

Mila giggled. "I know."

36

At home the Apple family was whole. Chloe snuggled up to Peter like a comforter and they all watched an old Disney movie together. Barry stayed next to Mila the whole time, quiet and calm. It was as if they had no worries in the world at that moment. Mila and Chloe giggled at the funny parts of the film, Peter and Barry were the usual stones.

When the movie was over, Mila started her homework and Chloe began preparing dinner. Peter came into the kitchen with her and started a conversation. He said, "Something's different about Barry. Do you think the conversation I had with him helped?"

"He's having bad dreams, babe."

"Well, that would explain why he was in bed this morning. He's never done that before. They must be pretty bad."

"He had a dream that the house was burning and Mila was stuck inside."

Peter shuddered. He said, "That's pretty bad."

"Yeah. He said that he thought he'd started the fire

in the dream and that he couldn't do anything to save her. It shook him up. He says he wants to be good now."

"That's surprising."

"I know. I'm wondering how long it'll last."

Chloe set the table and everyone sat down to eat meatloaf, green beans and mashed potatoes. The scent of the food filled the air, and when everyone was served, the meal went by without incident. The family talked and laughed, even Barry participated. The subject of a puppy came up.

Barry asked, "Poppa, can I have a puppy?"

Peter shook his head. He said, "No. I don't think that's a good idea."

Barry's face screwed into his trademark scowl. He said, "I'm gonna be good."

Peter said, "You haven't shown that yet, son. Besides that, I don't want a dog here. End of story."

Barry stood and stormed away, into his room. Peter and Chloe looked at each other, and Mila said, "Hey. He didn't throw his food on the floor."

The three of them chuckled. It was a new kind of day in the Apple household.

37

Thursday evening Peter began fixing Chloe's car. After the children were in bed she joined him in the driveway with a couple of beers. He took a moment to guzzle some of the cold beverage. Chloe loved the way he looked with his greasy hands and his ball cap on. She admired his strong, square jawline. When he took the beer away from his lips he leaned down and planted a wet kiss on her forehead.

Chloe wiped her forehead. She asked, "Do you think it'll be ready for tomorrow?"

"Oh yeah. It's nothing, sugar plum. I got the whole thing unbolted. All I've got to do now is pull it out and pop the other radiator in. It's a cakewalk."

"That's good. I don't want you to have to miss work."

"I wouldn't be missin' it much." Peter laughed. "I like it up there, but I don't love it."

"You should open your own shop. I keep telling you."

"Nah, I'm not ready for all that yet. I like punchin' in and punchin' out for now."

Chloe snuggled up against him. She said, "You're so good at working on anything. Especially cars. You should think about it."

"I will, sugar. For now, let me finish what I'm doing and I'll meet you inside."

Chloe gazed up into Peter's eyes. She said, "I love you, babe."

"You better, or I'm not gonna cuddle with you anymore."

Chloe gasped and feigned offense. Stepping back, she slapped Peter in the arm. She said, "You better cuddle with me, mister."

Peter laughed. "I will, sugar. You already know. I love you, too, babe."

Peter downed the rest of his beer after Chloe went inside. Leaning over the car's engine compartment, he started turning wrenches.

38

Friday came. Mila hadn't had any further complications with the red head boy. She felt vulnerable in the hallways, so she hurried from one class to the next without wasting much time. Her math teacher said, "This is the second day in a row that you're the first in class, Mila. Is something wrong between you and your friends?"

"No, I just don't feel like hanging out in the halls."

"That's unusual. Most of the children are reluctant to show."

"Well, I don't want to talk about it."

"If you decide you do, I'm a good listener."

"Thanks, Mrs. French. It's nothing really. I just don't want to see someone."

"A boy?"

"I'd rather not say."

"Ok. I'll leave it alone. You should know that you can't run away from problems forever. Eventually we all have to face what challenges us."

Mila wanted to believe otherwise. She was going to avoid the kid until she had no other choice. Knowing the school wasn't so big that she wouldn't see him again, she hoped that he would lose interest in her by the next time he saw her. Something in her gut told her she would have to deal with him soon.

The class began to fill. Sandra sat in the desk next to Mila. She looked at Mila with a smirk. She asked, "What are you doing?"

"Nothing. I'm waiting on class to start."

"Do you like that boy?"

Mila felt her skin tingle and goose bumps stood on her arm. She asked, "What boy?"

"Elvin Craig, the fifth grader. We saw you look at him and run away, so Veronica and I went to talk to him."

Mila's eyes were as wide as a deer's caught in headlights. Trying not to panic, her whole body began shaking. She asked, "What did you say to him?"

Sandra giggled. "Don't worry. We just told him you had a crush."

Mila's mouth went dry and she felt herself tremble harder inside. She asked, "Why would you do that?"

"We saw you look at him and turn to go the other way. You have a crush, right?"

Mila stood up, gathered her things, and left the classroom. She could hear Mrs. French calling out. "Mila where are you going?"

She ignored her teacher's voice, feeling nauseous when she entered the girls' restroom. Her fear had become a reality. Looking at herself in the mirror, tears began streaming down her pale cheeks. She considered leaving the school, wanting to run away and never come back. She could imagine the kids taunting her, and the boy—Elvin—torturing her. Leaving the bathroom, she headed for the exit. Turning down the north hallway, she walked into Principal Walker.

Principal Walker spotted Mila at about the same time. She said, "Young lady, aren't you supposed to be in class?"

Mila wiped her eyes. She said, "I don't feel well. I want to go home."

"I suppose you should be heading to the nurse's office if you don't feel well. It looked to me like you were heading for the front doors."

Mila shuddered. She said, "I just want to leave, Mrs. Walker."

"That's not how it works, Mila. It is Mila, right?"

"Yes."

Principal Walker clucked. She said, "Walking out of the school without telling anyone isn't the way to leave, Little Miss Apple. There are channels you must go through before leaving. Do you understand? Anarchy won't be tolerated. Principal Walker will not tolerate anarchy."

Mila felt chaotic. She said, "You're mean. I don't want to stay and you can't make me." She shook with anxiety and frustration.

Principal Walker said, "Do you want to be some kind of deviant? Like your brother? Come to my office and we'll call your parents."

Mila followed the principal. She didn't want to go

back to the classroom and she didn't want to stay at school. It didn't matter to her whether her parents were called or if she had to run away, she'd had enough for the day. Wiping her nose on her sleeve, she only wanted to be safe at home.

39

Chloe received the phone call about Mila while she prepared to leave for the doctor's appointment with Barry. She wasn't sure she'd be able to pick Mila up and make the appointment on time. She told the principal, "I'm going to pick her up, but I don't have time to stop and talk. I have somewhere to be."

"Well, Mrs. Apple, you must come inside and sign her release papers."

"Ok. That's fine. But we'll have to discuss anything else later."

"I suppose we could, Mrs. Apple, but Mila needs to know she can't leave the school every time she has a problem."

"Don't worry, Mrs. Walker, I'll have a talk with her. Right now I really need to get off this phone and be on my way. I'll be running late as it is."

"Very well, we'll be waiting for you."

Chloe hung up the phone and looked at Barry. He was sitting on the couch eating a pickle. She went to the fridge and pulled out a juice pack. She said, "Let's go, big guy. We've got to pick up your sister on the way."

Barry crunched his pickle. He said, "I heard."

Chloe inserted the packaged juice's straw and handed it to him. She said, "I hope we're not late. You won't be able to go back to school."

Barry put the straw in his mouth. He said, "Mmm, grape. I don't want to go back to school."

"I thought you wanted to be good."

"I do."

"Well, going to school is part of being good. Let's go."

40

Chloe pulled up in front of Clinton elementary and took Barry out of his car seat. They walked inside and went directly to the administration office. Mila was sitting in one of the little wooden chairs. When she saw her mother and brother walk in, she ran to her mother and hugged her waist. Chloe smoothed Mila's hair.

Chloe said, "We've got to get going, baby. We're going to be late."

Chloe looked at the secretary. She said, "Are there some papers I need to sign?"

"Oh, yes."

She stood from her desk and went to the counter in the room, with two pieces of paper. She spread them out in front of Chloe and showed her where to sign. She tapped her pen on the counter top and smiled at Mila and Barry. Chloe was overwhelmed by the flowery perfume the secretary was wearing, wondering if it was the same fragrance the principal used. She couldn't understand why some women felt compelled to bathe in perfume.

The secretary said, "Mrs. Walker was hoping to be

back in the office when you arrived. Do you have time to wait?"

Chloe felt frustration building. She said, "No. I explained to her over the phone that we would have to discuss this later. I have somewhere to be." She didn't like repeating herself.

The secretary didn't seem to be put off at all by Chloe's attitude. Smiling like a lunatic, she said, "Well then, have a good day." She looked at Mila. "I hope you feel better soon, sweetheart. Your grades are going to suffer if you miss too much class."

Mila said, "Thanks, Mrs. Coughlin."

The Apples left the school, and Chloe tried not to break too many laws on her way to the psychiatrist's office.

41

Sitting in front of Gabriella Payne was not as terrible as Chloe had expected. Gabriella was as gorgeous as Chloe remembered her being, but it didn't bother her the way it had when Peter had been with her. Mila and Barry played with stuffed animals on the floor while she spoke with the doctor.

Dr. Payne asked, "Would you like something to drink?"

"No, thank you."

"What about the children?"

Chloe turned. She asked Mila and Barry, "Are you two thirsty?"

While the kids waited for their juices, Dr. Payne asked, "How have things been since the last time I saw you?"

"They've been hectic. Barry has been in all types of trouble. We're here today because he assaulted a student with a metal lunch box."

Dr. Payne said, "He gave everybody a big scare recently, also. Didn't he?"

"Yes, he ran off and broke into someone's home."

"Why do you think he does things like that?"

"I was hoping you could tell me."

Dr. Payne looked over Chloe's shoulder at the children. She said, "I'm going to need to spend some time with Barry, alone. If that's okay."

"I don't have a problem with that. But I need a note for Barry to go back to school."

"I understand. It's not so simple though. You will need to commit to bi-monthly visits. The school is going to want to know you are actively seeking help."

"Yes, I want help. We can do bi-monthly."

"Okay, let me spend the rest of the hour with Barry, we'll go from there."

Chloe stood and exited the room with Mila. She was anxious, having Barry stay in the room alone with Gabriella. Feeling apprehensive about leaving, she also knew that if she didn't comply it would be that much longer before he went back to school and she might return to her job. Squeezing Mila's hand, she took a seat in the waiting room with the calm and polite secretary.

The secretary asked Mila, "Aren't you supposed to be in school, little one?"

Mila said, "I wasn't feeling well, so I left early. What's your name?"

"My name's Linda." And with a big smile on her face, Linda asked, "What's your name?"

"I'm Mila."

"It's very nice to meet you, Mila."

"It's nice to meet you. Do you have to be nice to everyone?"

"I think it's best to be nice to everyone."

"Hmm. There's this boy, and I know he's mean. Do you think I should be nice to him?"

"I think you should be nice to everyone. But if he's mean, maybe you should be nice and keep your distance."

Chloe asked, "Is that what the whole leaving school early thing was? You're avoiding a boy?"

"He's really mean and my friends told him I have a crush on him."

Chloe's eyes opened wide. She began fidgeting. She asked, "Do you?"

"No, Mommy. But now he thinks I do and he's probably going to do something mean. He'll probably start making fun of me in front of everyone." Mila's frown and tear-filled eyes broke Chloe's heart.

Linda said, "It's not good to run away from your responsibilities because of a potential bully, little one. Bullies are everywhere, and you would spend your whole life running if you tried to escape them all."

The hour passed and Dr. Payne opened her office door, standing in the entryway. She said, "Mrs. Apple, you can come back now."

Chloe stood with Mila and they went into the office. She saw Barry on the floor playing with the same stuffed animals he was playing with before she left. Mila went to join him and Chloe took a seat at the doctor's desk. Gabriella sat down and tapped her chin. They sat quietly for a moment. Chloe felt anxiety well up.

Dr. Payne said, "I assume Barry has told you about

his dreams?"

"Yes, he says he wants to be good."

"Right." Gabriella stared in the children's direction. She said, "Barry is a smart boy. I think he may be fabricating some of it. I think he may know how much trouble he's in and he's trying to find a way out."

Chloe was shocked. She asked, "At his age? Do you really think that's possible?"

"You would be surprised, Mrs. Apple. Most five-year-olds have very active imaginations. He still shows little remorse for the things he's done, but he wants you to believe that he doesn't want to be bad anymore. It's actually not all that uncommon."

"So you think he's going to go back to his old ways?"

"It's very likely. Although he is at a changing point, I don't think he's going to be a model of good behavior. Mind, he probably is having bad dreams, his reaction to them is more of a defense mechanism right now from what I gather. I think he wants everybody to believe he's going to be good. It's possible he could say anything that might get him out of trouble or gain sympathy."

Chloe began fidgeting. She asked, "What should I do?"

"I think you should monitor his behavior closely. Let me know if you notice anything unusual. I'm sure he's conflicted inside either way. I know that he knows he's been doing wrong. What we need is to see he actually realizes how wrong he is."

42

On the ride home, both Mila and Barry were quiet. The radio played softly, but not loud enough to drown out when Barry started making artificial flatulence with his mouth. Chloe and Mila looked at each other and both rolled their eyes.

Chloe wondered if Barry's good behavior streak was already running out. She wondered if he was doing what he was doing for a reaction. She leaned forward and turned the radio off, then adjusted the rearview to see Barry in his car seat. He was looking out his window seemingly in his own world.

Chloe said, "Barry, honey, could you stop that."

Barry looked at her and she expected a scowl on his face, his expression was placid. He asked, "Can we have ice cream?"

Chloe looked at Mila again. There was a sparkle in the young girl's light blue eyes and she was wearing a smirk. They had her on the ropes. Knowing her answer, she asked, "Why do you two deserve ice cream?"

Barry spoke without a moment's pause. "I went to the doctor and Mila doesn't feel well. I think ice cream would be good."

Chloe huffed. She said, "I guess. Just small cones though, I don't want you to ruin your appetites."

Mila clapped her hands and another check in the rearview revealed an almost manic looking smile on Barry's face. In that moment, just the briefest of moments, Chloe wondered if he was a maniac. It faded fast, and she told herself she was being paranoid. Turning the car around, she headed to the ice cream shop.

43

At home, Chloe busied herself with house duties
while Mila and Barry watched cartoons. Chloe felt
disturbed about the fact that Mila had left school early
because of a boy. Likewise, she was disturbed about the
psychiatrist's words concerning Barry. She tried to
empty her mind while folding laundry, working on
autopilot, when her cell phone rang, startling her.

Looking at the caller I.D., Chloe saw that it was
Rebecca. Chloe hadn't fielded many calls since she'd
left work. She loathed discussing her son's antics with
anyone. She decided to answer just as it was about to go
to voicemail.

"Hello."

"Hey, Beautiful. What are you doing?"

Chloe smiled into the phone. She said, "I'm doing
house-mom stuff. What are you up to?"

"I was just about to leave work and go take a long,
hot shower. Do you like hot showers?"

Chloe giggled. She asked, "Are you inviting me to
shower with you?"

"No. I wanted to invite you to drinks, you can come

over and take a shower if you want though."

"I don't know if I can go out tonight. There's a lot going on here."

"Why don't you talk to your hubby and call me back this evening."

"I guess I could."

"I'll be waiting to hear from you. Try to call me by eight, that way I can get ready. I'll pick you up if you want."

Chloe wasn't sure about having Rebecca over. She didn't know if she wanted Peter laying his eyes on the perfect specimen that she seemed to be. It was that jealous bone aching inside her that she could never successfully quiet. She thought about it so long, that Rebecca said, "Or, you can come to me, either way."

"That would probably be better." Chloe's ears were hot. She felt embarrassed by her thoughts

44

When Peter came in from work, Chloe and the children met him at the door. Barry and Mila ran to embrace their father whom they loved so much. He knelt down and welcomed the affection. Chloe stood in the foyer drying her hands with a dish towel. When Peter stood, he went to her and planted a kiss on her lips.

He asked, "What's for dinner?"

Chloe replied, "One of your favorites."

"Sugar plum, everything you cook is my favorite."

Chloe rolled her eyes. "So you say."

Peter laughed. He said, "You know it's true."

Chloe beamed. She said, "Three-cheese lasagna and garlic bread with a side of green beans."

"Mmm-mmm. It smells delicious. I'm going to get a quick shower and eat all that goodness."

"You better get a shower, dirty man. I need to talk to you about some things after dinner."

"Sure thing, sugar." He kissed her on her forehead and set off for the master bathroom.

Mila asked, "Are you going to tell him about me?"

"Sweetie, you know I have to."

"No, you don't, Mommy. It can be our secret."

"That's absurd, baby. He needs to know when you're having problems."

Mila pouted and walked away. Chloe felt horrible. Knowing how much Mila adored her father, she hated having to be the one telling him she was having issues, especially when Mila felt embarrassed by the problem. She looked down at Barry and took a deep breath.

She said, "Why do I always have to be the bad guy?"

"It's your job, Momma."

Chloe threw the dish rag on his head. She said, "Thanks a lot, mister."

45

When dinner was over and the children were tucked away in bed, Peter and Chloe sat down for their talk. Chloe began by telling him about the doctor visit. He didn't seem surprised to hear what Gabriella had to say about Barry. Chloe felt horrible about having to bring Mila up next. She wanted to avoid the conversation, but she knew that if she did—it would be wrong.

She sighed. She said, "Mila's having boy problems."

Peter's brow furrowed. He asked, "What kind of boy problems?"

"There's a boy at school she's trying to avoid. I picked her up early today because of it."

"Why would you do that?"

"Because, I was in a hurry. I didn't have time for a discussion. I just signed the papers and picked her up."

Peter exhaled loudly. He said, "She's going to think it's okay to run away from problems if you let her run every time she wants to avoid someone."

Chloe shook her head. She said, "I'm not trying to instill that in her. What was I supposed to do? I was in a hurry and she was trying to leave school without telling anyone at first. I couldn't just leave her there."

Peter felt saddened. He didn't want to make Chloe feel worse than she already did.

He said, "You did what you thought was right, I probably would have done the same."

He reached up and touched Chloe's cheek. He said, "You seem really stressed. I wish I knew how to ease your mind."

Chloe smiled. She said, "Rebecca called me earlier."

"What did she say?"

"She wanted to know if I could go have a drink with her tonight."

Peter asked, "Do you want to?"

"Kind of."

"Well, if you want to go you can. I'll watch the kids."

"Really?"

"Yeah, sugar plum. You go have a good time, try to relax. Do you work tomorrow?"

"I'm scheduled from eight until noon."

"Try not to drink too much then. You don't want to feel like crap in the morning."

Chloe rolled her eyes. "A lecture?"

Peter laughed. He said, "I'm just looking out for you, sugar."

"I'm a big girl."

"Well, if you do get buzzed, you can call me and stay at your friend's if you need to."

"You know I don't drink much. I'll be home. I need to call Rebecca before it gets much later. I've got to get ready, also."

She left the table to call her friend.

46

Pulling into Rebecca's apartments, Chloe felt chills run up and down her spine. She hadn't been out drinking without Peter in a long time. Feeling a little shocked that he'd actually agreed to let her go, she checked her makeup in the rearview. Even suggesting she stayed the night if she needed! She shook her head. Knowing how stressed out she'd been lately, he was being open to let her relax and have a good time. Thinking about how sweet he was, she tried to think of ways she could make him feel good while she listened to the phone ring in her ear.

Rebecca picked up. She said, "I know, you're here."

Chloe looked around at the apartment building. She didn't see anyone in any of the windows, or any doors open. She asked, "How did you know I was here?"

Rebecca laughed in a seductive and sultry way. She said, "Baby, I estimated your time of arrival and then glanced at the camera a few times."

"Camera?"

"Yeah, I've got surveillance cameras up. I can see all around me."

Chloe looked around the eaves of the building and spotted the tiny devices after close inspection. She asked, "Why do you need cameras? Are you a drug dealer?"

Rebecca laughed again, this time with enthusiasm, amusement.

She said, "You're hilarious. No, I'm not a drug dealer. I guess I'm just a paranoid. Now, are you going to come in or are we going to stay on the phone all night?"

Chloe could see Rebecca standing in her apartment's doorway now. The slim beauty was in a short black low-cut dress that clung to her body with a silky shine. She was smiling her dazzling white smile and waiving for Chloe to come inside. Chloe hung up the phone and exited the car, feeling self-conscious in her blue, knee-length, long-sleeve number. She couldn't imagine being able to rival her friend's looks.

Greeting Chloe with a hug, Rebecca took her hand, leading her into the cozy apartment. It was immaculate. The kind of clean and tidy that was a myth in Chloe's world. The furniture was all modern black and white pieces down to the lamps and shades. There was a fireplace with a full-size grizzly fur in front of it. The head was still attached to the bear rug. Rebecca noticed the long pause Chloe took inspecting the pelt.

Rebecca said, "I shot him myself."

Chloe's eyes went wide. She covered her mouth with her hand. She said, "You didn't."

Rebecca smiled wide with the curious look in her

eyes, as if she was analyzing Chloe for a meal. She said, "I shot him in British Columbia. He was almost nine feet tall and a thousand pounds give or take."

Chloe felt shocked. She couldn't imagine the petite and proper woman standing in front of her wielding the kind of weapon it would take to kill something the size of what was now a large throw rug. She took in the three or four inch claws and shiny hair once again. It looked like a former ferocious beast with its large teeth showing in what was now a perpetual snarl.

Chloe asked, "How long have you been a hunter? It seems so odd."

Rebecca snorted. She said, "Why's it odd, baby? Because I'm a woman?"

"No. I didn't mean it like that."

"Well. We can talk about it later. I've got to call a cab and we have a city to blow through. I'll tell you all types of wild things before the night's over, if you're lucky."

Chloe sat in one of the plush arm chairs. Rebecca swayed off into one of the back rooms to finish getting ready. She was only out of sight for a moment when she returned. She said, "There's drinks in the refrigerator if you want one. Wine coolers and beer, white and red wine in the chiller. I can get you something if you like."

Chloe felt amused. She asked, "Do you have anything besides wine?"

"Sure. You want a tequila sunrise?" She smiled her killer smile.

Chloe said, "I'll take some tequila by itself. A shot."

Rebecca's curious look returned. She said, "You can have it any way you want it, girlfriend."

47

The cab pulled to the curb of what looked like an abandoned building, except it had a neon sign above some very plain double doors. Two men stood outside in suits. The neon sign was lit bright pink, with a purple border. The sign read, 'The Promiscuous Cat'. Chloe stepped out on the sidewalk, Rebecca stepped out behind her. Chloe could hear the driving, musical bass beat coming from inside the walls.

Rebecca took Chloe's hand. She said, "Let's get inside."

Chloe followed Rebecca's lead and they went to the doors. One of the oversized goons opened the door. He said, "Ladies."

Rebecca smiled. She said, "Thanks, Stephen."

Stephen smiled and winked. Chloe felt nervous going into the club, having no idea what to expect. She asked Rebecca, "Do you come here a lot?"

"Only when I have someone to show off."

Chloe blushed. There were black curtains in the small hallway through the entrance. When they passed through the curtains Chloe felt awestruck. The club was immaculate. Chandeliers hung from the ceiling and the lighting was low. There were groups of people at tables in the center and a stairway leading to a balcony. She could see people on the balcony looking down to where she and Rebecca stood.

House music played loudly; Chloe could feel it in her chest. She could see the packed dance floor at the back of the club. There were women grinding, gyrating and dancing in every type of obscene manner. Chloe realized it was all women. She looked around at the tables and they were all occupied by women. Some of them were kissing. Others were talking closely and gazing into each other's eyes.

She spotted a man in the crowd. He was carrying a tray with drinks on it. Chloe looked at Rebecca. She asked, "Is this a 'women's only' club?" She had to strain her voice over the music.

Rebecca said, "Yeah, baby. These are the good ones. Let's get a table."

Without another word, Rebecca pulled Chloe into the crowd.

48

Chloe felt nervous sitting in the red booth with Rebecca. She hadn't imagined a women's club looking like this one. There were a few women with short hair, in men's clothes. The whole scene was unusual to Chloe. She began fidgeting. Rebecca looked at her with the curious look she did so well.

She asked, "Are you nervous?"

Chloe bit her lip and took another look around. "It's just so odd being in a place like this. Do you like women?"

Rebecca smiled and Chloe wouldn't have been surprised if the beautiful creature licked her lips in response. She said, "I like men and women. Don't you?"

Chloe emitted a nervous laugh. "Probably not in the same way you do."

A server approached the table. "Hello ladies, I'm Bill and I'll be your server tonight. Can I get you anything?"

Rebecca beamed and ordered some white wine for herself and Chloe. The buff server seemed pleased to assist. Chloe asked, "Are all the staff musclebound men?"

Rebecca laughed. She said, "Pretty much, baby. Do you like them?"

"They're nice to look at, but I have a man."

"What's your husband look like?"

Chloe fished her phone out of her clutch purse and showed Rebecca a picture. Rebecca said, "Wow. You got a hunk of a man."

Chloe's ears became hot.

"Yeah, I know."

The server returned with the wine and Chloe took a sip. She said, "Mmm, you're good. This is delicious." The sweet liquid seemed to dance on her tongue.

Rebecca asked, "What's going on with your son?"

Chloe put her glass down. "Everything's fine. He's going to be okay."

"You know, I saw the evening news the other night. Looked like he was being a real handful."

Blood rushed to Chloe's face. She began to fidget. She asked, "Do you think everyone at work saw it?"

"I don't know. I think there's a good possibility some of them did."

Chloe bit her lip. Rebecca said, "You know, you're real cute when you're nervous or embarrassed, or whatever this is."

Chloe rolled her eyes. She said, "Please, don't start now, Rebecca. It's not funny."

"What's funny is that your son is the youngest burglar I ever heard of. How adorable."

Chloe huffed. "It's not adorable. He's been a little

monster, and now everyone knows."

"It's not that bad, baby. He's probably going to make a great felon." Rebecca laughed. She continued, "Unless someone shows him the right way."

"I'm trying to teach him right. He hasn't been listening to me."

"Don't feel bad. I think most kids are rotten."

"How can you say that? Some are good. Mila's practically an angel."

Rebecca smirked and raised an eyebrow. She said, "You just wait. That little angel could turn out to be a bigger problem than the little felon, in the future."

"I doubt it."

"Do you want to dance?"

Chloe looked at the dance floor and the throng of body rubbing women. She said, "I don't think so. I'd rather just sit here and drink."

Rebecca gave the curious look. "Suit yourself. I'm going to go shake my butt." She stuck her tongue out and Chloe noticed for the first time that it was pierced. Rebecca stood and swayed towards the dance floor. Chloe took another sip of wine and thought to herself what a peculiar friend she'd made.

49

The ride back to Rebecca's was interesting. Rebecca leaned over and put her head on Chloe's shoulder. She said, "I hope we're friends forever."

Chloe giggled. "I'm not very interesting. I wouldn't even dance with you."

"You will next time."

"I don't know if there'll be a next time."

Rebecca sat up with a disturbed look on her face. She asked, "Why not? Didn't you have fun?"

"It was fun. Different. I just don't know if Peter will be comfortable with me frequenting a club like that."

"It's better than a regular club. There aren't groups of men trying to slobber on you at this one."

"I guess that's true. But there's plenty of women who want to do things."

"Yeah, but baby, you're with me. No one's stealing you from me."

Chloe rolled her eyes and giggled. She said, "You're a real character. I'm glad I didn't have much to drink. I'm ready to get home and shower. I've got to be at the bakery at eight in the morning."

"Me, too." Rebecca exhaled loudly. "I only got that job for something to do. I'm glad I did, because I met you."

"I'm sure you don't have a problem meeting people."

"You'd be surprised. I don't like most people."

"You seem like a sociable person."

"Well. I did a lot of moving around. Most people get on my nerves."

The cab pulled into Rebecca's apartments and the girls exited the vehicle. Rebecca asked, "Do you want to come inside? Maybe have one more drink before you go?"

Chloe looked at her watch. She said, "It's already really late, almost two in the morning. I think I should be going."

Rebecca hugged Chloe and gave her a kiss on the cheek. She said, "We can go out anytime you want, I'll be calling to invite."

Chloe giggled. "I'll be expecting your calls."

Rebecca stood on the sidewalk and watched Chloe get in her car. Chloe fished her cellphone from her purse and called Peter. When he answered, Chloe could tell he was wide awake from the sound of his voice. She felt a pang of guilt for keeping him up.

She said, "You wanted me to call when I was on my way home. I'm on my way."

"Have you had much to drink? Are you okay to drive?"

"I'm okay. I didn't drink much."

"How was your night?"

"I'll tell you about it when I get there, babe. It was good."

"Okay. I love you. I'll see you when you get here."

"I love you, too."

Chloe disconnected and waived at Rebecca. Pulling out of the parking lot, she headed home. On the way there she thought about her night out with her new friend. The whole evening was odd to her and somehow refreshing. She turned up the radio and pop music emanated from the speakers. Rolling her window halfway down, she began belting out the chorus to the popular song with a smile on her face.

50

When Chloe arrived home, she saw Peter sitting on the front porch, smoking a cigarette—in his pajamas. Stepping out of the car, she shook her head. She said, "I thought you'd given those up."

Peter flicked the cigarette into the yard and stood. "I bought a pack on the way home from work. That's the first one I've smoked."

He embraced her and they went inside. Peter asked, "How was your night? Any guys try hitting on you?"

"Not exactly."

Entering their bedroom, Chloe began to undress. Peter said, "Well, tell me about it. Did you have fun?"

"It was okay. Rebecca's a real character."

"Where'd you go?"

"A place called 'The Promiscuous Cat'."

Peter looked like he was in deep thought. He said, "I've never heard of it."

"Yeah, I don't think they advertise. I'd never heard of it before tonight. It's a women's club; the only men there were the servers."

"Oh. Kind of dull?"

"Not really. It was loud and there was a lot of dancing. I didn't do any dancing though. Most of the women there were couples."

"You were kind of a couple. Did Rebecca dance?"

"Yeah, she got out there. She's braver than me."

"You could have gotten out there. It's no big deal. I feel a little better you weren't in some place fending off men all night."

"I guess. I didn't want to give Rebecca any ideas or the wrong impression though."

Peter looked confused. He asked, "Does she make you uncomfortable?"

"No. Not at all. It's not like that."

"Then what is it?"

"I guess I'm worried she's going to make a move on me."

Peter ran his fingers through his hair. He asked, "Is she into women?"

"Yeah. Women and men. I really like her and I don't want to be uncomfortable with her. If she tried to do something like kiss me I might not want to be around her anymore."

"I don't think it'd be that big of a deal, sugar plum. If something like that happened I'm sure she would be able to respect your boundaries, if she values your friendship. You might want to make it clear though. Instead of waiting for her to ruin everything."

"You're right. I'm going to talk to her tomorrow at work. I just want to take a shower and crash out right now. I'm worn out."

Chloe stripped off her undergarments and went to the bathroom.

51

The alarm clock went off at 7 o'clock. Chloe's arm flailed around the nightstand until she found the kill button to hush the irritating noise of it. Sitting up, she realized Peter was missing. Chloe stumbled into the bathroom and washed her face, then picked up her tooth brush. The scent of bacon wafted in and she realized Peter had wakened early and was busy cooking breakfast. Smiling while she brushed her teeth, she thought how much she loved her husband.

Walking into the kitchen, she could see utter chaos. Peter had somehow managed to get the children up and they were helping prepare breakfast with smiles on their faces. Barry stood covered in flour, Mila stood on a stool at the kitchen island pouring orange juice into four tall glasses. Mila was the first to notice Chloe standing in the doorway. She said, "Aww. We wanted to give you breakfast in bed."

Peter and Barry turned to face Chloe from their pancake station and waved. Crossing the room, Chloe approached Mila and kissed her forehead. Chloe said, "You're very sweet, honey. I love you all so much."

Mila smiled. She said, "We love you, too, Mommy. Sit down and we can bring it to you. Please."

Chloe rolled her eyes. She said, "Okay."

Sitting at the table, Chloe watched her man and children work, thinking to herself how nice it is when the people you love want to pamper you. Before long they were all sitting at the table eating. Chloe asked Peter, "What do you have planned for the day?"

Peter smiled. He said, "We have a special day planned. Barry's going to make forgive-me cards for the boy that he hurt at school and the family's house he intruded. We're gonna get him a haircut, then make the rounds."

Chloe felt elated. She said, "That's great. I'm so proud of you both."

Mila said, "Hey. What about me?"

Chloe giggled. She said, "I'm proud of you, too, sweetie. I hope everything goes well with all y'alls adventures today."

Barry said, "We're up early to tell you to have a good day at work."

Chloe felt tears welling in her eyes. She said, "That's very thoughtful, honey. I love you all so much."

Mila said, "It's okay, Mommy. We know."

The kids were on the living room floor making cards when Chloe left for work. Arriving at the bakery in a good mood, Rebecca pulled in the space beside her. The women met each other behind their vehicles. Rebecca said, "You look like you're in a good mood."

"I am. I woke up to my family making breakfast for

me. Isn't that nice?"

"Adorable. Are you ready to go into this hen house and face the clucking?"

Chloe rolled her eyes, then giggled. She said, "You're so bad, Rebecca. Such a way with words."

Rebecca peered at her with the curious look in her eyes Chloe had come to expect. Rebecca said, "You're not hung over. My head is pounding."

Chloe began digging in her purse. She said, "I've got Ibuprofen somewhere in here."

Rebecca touched Chloe's arm and raised her eyebrows. She said, "I took something already, baby. Let's just get in here and get this day over with. I need a friggin' drink."

Chloe smirked. "You're going to start drinking at noon?"

"Damn right I am."

Chloe noticed a shine on Rebecca's neck that she hadn't noticed before. It appeared to be a scar. She asked, "What happened to your neck?"

"Well. Aren't we observant early in the morning?"

"I'm sorry. I never noticed it before. "

"I'm going to be the curious one. Remember?"

"I said I was sorry."

"Don't be. It's from a hunting accident."

"It's still hard to believe you hunt."

"I'll take you hunting with me some time. Now, let's go."

"Okay."

Entering the building, it was obvious all the women

inside had been watching them in the parking lot. Julissa approached. She said, "You're both late. Chloe, since you just started back, it's unacceptable. You're fired." Julissa's attitude was stern.

Chloe said, "I'm ten minutes late. You can't fire me."

"I can and I did. Rebecca, you have work to do in the back, and Chloe, if you would—vacate the premises."

Chloe began crying and exited the building. Rebecca said to Julissa, "That was cruel. You know you didn't fire her because she was late."

Julissa glared. The normally jolly, smiling and accepting person had turned into a wench. Rebecca wanted to punch her in the face. Julissa said, "You can get to work or go home with her. I don't care which option you choose, but choose quickly."

Rebecca felt bad for not chasing Chloe into the parking lot to console her. She looked out the window and Chloe was in her car, leaving the bakery in a hurry. Rebecca's heart sank knowing how hurt her friend was. Anger welled inside her and she turned to Julissa.

"I'm staying."

52

Arriving home, Chloe sat in the driveway for a few minutes gathering herself. She knew her family was probably still in the living room making cards. Looking in the visor mirror, she fixed her make-up and stilled herself. The thoughts going through her head were causing a whirlwind of emotion. Feeling awful, she considered leaving.

The front door opened and Peter stood in his pajamas, watching her. She could read the concern on his face. Stepping out the vehicle, leaning against it, she pouted in disgust. Peter called out. "What happened, sugar? Are you alright?"

Chloe didn't want to look towards him, worried she might start crying again. She looked at the ground. "I got fired."

She watched Peter approach from her peripheral vision. Embracing her, he kissed her forehead. He said, "Great. You get to spend the day with us."

Chloe smiled. He was trying to make her feel better, and she loved him for it. She said, "I really wanted to work."

Peter put his chin on top of her head. "You'll find another job, sugar plum. You don't need that bakery."

She said, "She fired me because I was late. I know that's not why though."

"Try not to think about it, sugar. They don't deserve you up there."

Chloe huffed, feeling a little better in Peter's arms, but still hurt. She said, "I embarrassed myself. I cried and ran out."

Peter squeezed her tighter. "It's okay. You're a girl."

Chloe pushed him away and smirked. She said, "Hey, mister. What's that supposed to mean?"

Peter laughed. He said, "You know what it means." He held his arm out for her to grab on to, and said, "We've got a good day ahead of us, sugar. Let's get in a light mood." Chloe took his arm and they went inside to help with the forgive-me cards.

53

Excited to have her mother along for the ride, Mila asked, "Will you sit in the back with me, Mommy?"

Chloe felt loved, she began to forget about her frustration from the bakery. "Sure. If your daddy will move your brother's car seat."

Peter grumbled disapproval, but he moved the seat. Chloe sat in the back and Mila took her hand, smiling. Feeling overwhelmed with joy, she squeezed Mila's small hand. It didn't matter that the women at the bakery didn't like her. She knew her family loved her. No amount of ugliness could keep her down with her daughter fighting for her attention.

At the barber's Barry sat still and patient while getting his haircut. He usually didn't make conversation while he was in the chair, but today he smiled and told his hair stylist all about the plans for the day. With his hair cut and lollipop in his mouth, he waved goodbye and took his father's hand. His hair stylist, Trina, waved. She said, "Good luck with your apologies, little man."

Peter drove slowly in the prominent neighborhood

where Steven Whitaker's family lived. The homes were towering examples of Victorian masterpieces, with the occasional modern monstrosity. The yards appeared meticulously maintained. They pulled into a driveway with a large wrought iron gate and brick wall. Steven Whitaker's residence.

The buzzer at the gate had a red light lit on a key pad, and several other buttons, next to a speaker. Peter rolled down his window and pressed a button labeled 'talk'. The little light turned green, and in a few short seconds, a man's voice echoed through the speaker. The man said, "Whitaker residence. How can I help you?"

Peter cleared his throat. He said, "We're looking for Steven Whitaker, sir. I'm Peter Apple. My family and I are here to make an apology."

The man's voice became agitated. He said, "Your family isn't welcome here. I suggest you leave or we'll call the police."

A woman's voice came from the background. She said, "Roger. Don't act like that. Let them in and hear what they have to say."

The man's voice sounded like a mild whine when he spoke again. He said, "Claire, I don't want these people in my home. Look what that boy did to Steven's face."

Claire said, "They're here to make an apology, Robert. You know it'll probably make Stevie feel better. He has to go to school with this boy."

"We'll put him in private school."

"No. Now let them in."

Roger said, "Come in then. You better not cause any trouble."

Peter turned red in the face and Chloe gripped Mila's hand as the large wrought iron fence opened. At this point no one in the car wanted to go in, but they had already committed. Peter drove slowly into the interior of the property. When they parked in the front of the home, the Whitakers were already at the door waiting.

Peter exited the vehicle and let Barry out. Chloe exited the vehicle with Mila by her side, latched on like they were attached at the hip. The Whitakers stood watching them approach. Steven's father, Roger, had an unforgiving look in his eyes. It wasn't difficult to read his mistrust. Steven stood by his father's side like a scared bear cub, his eye almost swollen shut from Barry's blow.

Steven's mother, Claire, was the first to speak. She said to Chloe, "I'm Claire Whitaker." She stretched out her hand.

Chloe took her hand. She said, "I'm Chloe Apple. Barry has something to give Steven."

Peter looked at Barry. He said, "Go ahead, son. Give Steven what you brought him."

Barry approached Steven and held out the card he made for him. Steven flinched, then realized Barry wasn't going to hurt him. Tension filled the air. Steven reached out and took the card. Chloe and Peter sighed with relief. Barry said, "It's a forgive-me card. My dad helped me make it. I'm sorry for what I did. Will you forgive me?"

Steven opened the card and his good eye bulged. He said, "There's a puppy picture in here. I love puppies."

"Yeah, my dad helped me glue it there. I love puppies, too."

Steven smiled. He said, "Do you want to see my puppy pictures? I've got a lot."

"Sure."

"Follow me."

The boy's ran inside together. Claire said, "I guess that settles it. He's forgiven. Now, how about a cup of tea?"

Chloe looked at Peter, he shrugged his shoulders. Chloe said to Claire, "We can't stay long. There's a few other things we have to do today."

Mrs. Whitaker said, "It's fine. One cup and I'll let you go."

Chloe began to worry about the woman's disposition. Thoughts of poisoned liquid swam through her mind. Shaking off the negativity, she followed Mrs. Whitaker into the large home. The first thing she noticed was the smell. It smelled sterile, like bleach and other scented cleaning chemicals. The home was immaculate, bright and full of paintings and antiques.

Mrs. Whitaker led them into a sitting area, then turned to Mr. Whitaker. She said, "Why don't you show Mr. Apple your parlor, dear? We're going to girl talk in here." She winked at Chloe.

When Mr. Whitaker and Peter were out of sight, Mrs. Whitaker said, "I'll get the tea, girls. Have a seat and I'll be right back."

Chloe and Mila sat down and observed their surroundings. Mila said, "Look how big the windows are, Mommy! They have a fire place, too."

Mrs. Whitaker returned with a tray. It had a ceramic tea pot on it and there were three little teacups. She put it on the coffee table and poured into the tiny cups. Chloe felt relaxed, but the tea setup was strange to her. Almost like the ceramic set with little flowers painted on it was a child's playthings. Mrs. Whitaker opened a small box containing sugar cubes. She asked, "How many lumps?" She looked from Chloe to Mila.

Chloe said, "I'll take one."

Mila asked, "Can I have two, Mommy?"

Mrs. Whitaker answered before Chloe could open her mouth. She said, "Of course you can have two, dear. Aren't you just precious in your little pink outfit?"

She dropped two sugar cubes in Mila's cup. Mila looked at her mother inquisitively. Chloe smiled and rolled her eyes. Mila stifled a giggle. Mrs. Whitaker handed them both their cups and took a seat in the brown leather chair next to the couch. Mila took a sip of her tea. She said, "This is really good, ma'am."

"Thank you, precious."

The flush in Mrs. Whitaker's cheeks made Chloe wonder if the woman was overheating. The temperature in the home was moderate and she felt comfortable, herself. She said, "You have such a beautiful complexion, Mrs. Whitaker."

"Oh, thank you, Chloe. Please, call me Claire."

Chloe wanted to ask her if she was hot, but she didn't want to be rude. Mila said, "Your cheeks are really red." Leave it to a child to point out the obvious.

Mrs. Whitaker said, "Yes, dear. I flush easily."

Mila replied with a simple, "Oh."

Mrs. Whitaker said, "We don't take many guests here." She laughed. "The ones we do take seldom return."

Chloe smiled. She said, "I can't imagine why not."

Mrs. Whitaker looked like she was in deep thought for a moment. She said, "I'm not much for entertainment. I take care of the house, Stevie and my husband. My husband is a writer and he's always working on something."

Chloe felt morose hearing the woman's tone. She asked, "What types of things does your husband write?"

"Well, let's see. He writes novels and short stories mostly. He didn't make much the first decade we were together."

Chloe looked around at the lavish surroundings. She said, "It looks like he's doing very well now."

"Yes, he is. The man won't buy anything himself, though. I bought everything you see, with his money of course. It's a chore getting him to leave the house. Guess what's in the garage."

Chloe didn't want to play a guessing game. She said, "I don't know."

"I'll tell you. There's a brand new Mercedes SUV. Do you know what's parked beside it?"

Chloe wanted to roll her eyes, she managed to

maintain her composure. The picture in her mind becoming clearer as to why they didn't have much repeat company. She asked, "What?"

"A nineteen eighty-nine Toyota pickup. It's got faded paint and squeals the whole time its running. Can you believe that?"

Chloe looked at Mila, who seemed equally stressed. Chloe said, "I wonder what the boys are up to."

Mrs. Whitaker snorted. She asked, "Which? Big or small?"

Chloe didn't often refer to Peter as a boy and she was slightly put off by the woman's tone when she made the comment. She said, "I'm talking about Barry and Steven. Do you think we can check on them?"

Mrs. Whitaker put her cup down. She said, "Heavens, let's go take a look."

54

Mrs. Whitaker led Chloe and Mila upstairs to Steven's room. The door was open and the boys could be seen from the hallway. Barry had a plastic plane in his hand. He was holding it above his head like it was in flight. Mila and Chloe marveled at Steven's room. It was filled with model aircraft. There were planes hanging from the ceiling and covering the walls. Where there weren't planes there were images of puppies. It was a little boy's paradise.

Chloe said to Barry, "Honey, we have to go."

Barry looked up from play, as if peering at her from another world. He said, "Momma, we just got here."

Chloe said, "Baby, we have other places to go. Have you forgotten?" Chloe bit her lip.

Barry said, "They'll be there, Momma. I just wanna play."

Looking around Steven's room it was apparent why Barry wanted to stay so badly. Mila said, "Mommy, look at all the planes on the ceiling!"

Mrs. Whitaker said, "Stevie loves to build planes with his father."

Chloe said to Barry, "Let's go, sweetie. Maybe we can come back some other time."

Steven smiled, infectiously. Chloe was glad the boys were getting along and felt terrible that she was breaking up the party. Mrs. Whitaker said, "That would be wonderful. You can come back any time you like."

Barry put the plane he was playing with on the floor. He asked, "Are we really coming back?"

"One day, sweetie. For now, we have things to do."

Chloe wondered how Peter's encounter was going. She asked Mrs. Whitaker, "Do you think you could let my husband know we're ready?"

Mrs. Whitaker pressed an intercom button next to the interior of Steven's door. She said into the intercom, "Roger, dear. Mrs. Apple is ready to go."

A few seconds later, Roger responded, "Okay, we'll meet you in the foyer."

The group met at the house's entrance and everyone said their goodbyes. To Chloe's surprise, Barry and Steven hugged. Elated at how well the apology had gone over, Chloe felt a warm feeling inside. Peter seemed to be in a good mood, also. She wanted to hear the details about his conversation with Mr. Whitaker.

Barry was in high spirits. He said, "I'm glad Steven liked my card." He looked at his father. "Do you think the other people will forgive me, too?"

Peter smiled. He said, "Son, as long as you're doing the right thing, it doesn't matter who accepts, really. You can feel good you're doing the right thing. That's what matters."

55

When the Apple family pulled in front of 2001 Clarice St., Peter looked more closely at the residence Barry had intruded upon than he had in passing the week before. There were broken toys in the yard and a bag of trash that was split open, showing its odious contents like a crime scene victim with his insides laid out, abandoned in a wasteland-remnant of what used to be a flower bed—now neglected and barren.

Peter shut the engine off and the family sat quietly for a moment. Mila broke the silence. She said to Barry, "You shouldn't have gone in this place, boo-boo."

Barry said, "I wanted to play."

Peter asked Barry, "Are you ready to go tell these people you're sorry?"

Barry looked at his hands and began fidgeting. Peter hadn't ever seen him so nervous. The way he behaved reminded him of Chloe. He reached over and ran his fingers through Barry's hair. He said, "Let's get it over with, son."

Barry smiled. He said, "I hope they're nice here. I really am sorry."

Chloe said, "We know you are, sweetie. Just remember what your daddy told you. Even if they don't accept your apology, you're doing the right thing. That's what matters."

"Okay, Momma. I'm ready."

The family exited the vehicle and went to the door as a group. They stood on the porch and looked at each other knowingly. Mila fanned her nose and crinkled her face. The odor of rotting trash was almost unbearable, so thick in the air that it had a taste. The emanating funk felt like mildew in their lungs.

Peter gave the door a few short but powerful raps. A commotion came from inside. The sound of something falling to the floor with a metallic clang and a man yelling. Impossible to make out what was being said … the family stood in nervous anticipation.

The door opened and there stood a skinny, balding man, with dirty, wrinkled clothes that matched the ambience of the unwelcoming lawn. He smelled of whiskey and had a cigarette with a disturbingly long ash hanging out of his mouth. A stench of vomit radiated from his clothing and wafted out of the house. It was hard for Peter to believe Barry had spent any amount of time in the residence.

Peter asked, "Are you Mr. Bannister?"

The man croaked, "I'm Kaleb," without reaching for or removing the cigarette. The ash fell off the tip and 'Kaleb' didn't blink.

Peter said, "We're looking for the owner of this residence."

"I'm the owner. Kaleb fucking Bannister."

Peter felt uncertain about the mess of a human being in front of him. He didn't appreciate the foul language or odor, either. Chloe asked, "Did we come at a bad time?"

The man looked at Chloe like she was some sort of three-eyed green alien. His dark brown, almost black and beady eyes made her skin crawl. Kaleb said, "When the hell is a good time lady? What the fuck do you people want?"

Anger swelled in Peter's being. He wanted to knock the teeth out of this dirty degenerate's filthy mouth. Peter said, "We came to give you an apology. Our son got into your house earlier in the week and he made you this card to apologize."

Kaleb raised his eyebrows. He said, "A damn card. You should be bringing me a wad of cash, all the damage that little prick did. Who the fuck breaks in and takes a shit on your floor. Get the fuck off my porch or I'll get a shovel."

Kaleb slammed the door so hard Chloe and Mila's hair stirred. Peter wanted to shout profanities, but he always tried to keep his cool, especially in front of the children. He knelt down next to Barry. The girls were in shock. Mila said to Barry, "That guy was really mean. What did he act like when he caught you?"

Barry said, "He was yelling and I ran out the house. The police found me running from him."

Peter asked, "Is that why you were so nervous, Buddy?"

"Yeah."

He looked down at Barry's tiny hands. The frightened child was holding the card so tightly that he was creasing it. Peter gently took the card. He said, "It was a brave thing you did coming here, son. It was the right thing. We'll put this in the mailbox and don't you worry if he appreciates it. I'm proud of you."

Peter took Barry's hand and the family left the porch, heading towards the car. Stopping at the mailbox, Peter placed the card inside. Everyone loaded into the vehicle and Barry watched the house disappear from sight. Mila said, "Mommy, I feel sorry for that man. He seemed miserable."

Chloe replied, "You're probably right, sweetie. Mean people are usually miserable. That's why they don't care about making anyone else sad."

56

The Apple family pulled into the parking lot of Barry's favorite restaurant. Barry's excitement made Chloe feel light and the rest of the family relax. He bounced back from the uncomfortable encounter well. Everyone exited the vehicle and before they went inside, Chloe's phone began to ring. She looked at the screen and saw it was Rebecca.

Chloe said to the family, "You guys go ahead without me, I'm going to take this outside."

Peter said, "Sure thing, sugar plum. We'll see you in there."

They went in, Barry practically jumping up and down and Mila attached to her father's arm, hand in hand. Chloe answered the phone. Rebecca said, "I'm sorry I didn't go after you earlier."

Chloe repressed her urge to say anything mean to Rebecca about anyone. She said, "It wasn't your fault. I didn't expect you to give up your job for me, you don't owe me that."

"You know, they all act like they have no abnormalities in their lives up here. They think they're perfect and it gets on my nerves, especially after the way you were treated today. I just want to do something horrible."

Chloe sighed. She said, "There's nothing to do. They're not going to change. I see now how judgmental and vindictive they are."

Rebecca said, "Baby, we can all be vindictive. What are you up to now? Want to get a drink?"

Chloe laughed. She said, "Crazy woman, it's barely noon."

"Yeah, I know. There's a happy hour downtown I frequent."

Chloe felt concerned her friend may be an alcoholic. She said, "I'm with my family. We've been running errands all morning, I'll have to take a rain check."

"What about tonight?" A sadness in Rebecca's voice made Chloe feel awkward. She didn't want Rebecca to be sad; she liked her.

Chloe said, "Maybe next weekend." Then she had a thought. She felt apprehensive about the thought because she was concerned about Peter meeting the gorgeous woman. Pushing her paranoias and jealousy issues aside, she asked, "Do you want to come to my house for dinner, Sunday?"

Rebecca exclaimed, "Yes! Would I be a bother?" Chloe could envision the wide smile her friend wore at the moment.

She said, "You wouldn't be a bother at all. I'm going to warn you though, my house is very modest and my kids can be heathens."

"Baby, I *was* a heathen. We'll get along just fine."

Chloe did her best to ignore the nervous feeling in the pit of her stomach.

57

Peter and Chloe woke early Sunday morning and busied themselves getting Barry and Mila ready for church. Bacon, eggs and toast being cooked, seared and baked, filled the house with delicious smells. The family sat at the table making light conversation while Chloe finished up and prepared to serve them.

A hard knock on the front door startled the whole group. Peter and Chloe looked at each other puzzled and concerned. Peter stood from the table. He said, "Go ahead and serve the food. I'll see who that is and be right back."

Chloe began filling his plate, then giving the children portions. Whoever was at the door was impatient. They started to knock again before Peter could reach the knob. He answered the door and two men stood confidently with dark sunglasses, slacks and dress shirts. The badges on their hips looked polished and stood out almost as much as the guns on their opposite hips.

The man to Peter's left had a stern look on his face. It was hard to read either of them, through their dark glasses. Peter asked, "Can I help you, officers?"

The one on the right, who looked younger by a decade, pulled a small notepad and pen from his pocket. The officer on the left said, "I'm Sergeant Sanders and this is Detective Jacks. We're looking for Chloe Apple. Is this the correct residence?"

"I'm Peter Apple, Chloe's my wife."

Detective Jacks scribbled on his notepad. He asked, "Is your wife home?"

Peter felt apprehensive. He asked, "May I ask what this is about?"

Sergeant Sanders said, "There's a situation at your wife's former place of employment. We need to ask her a few questions."

"What's the situation?" Peter's concern made his stomach turn.

Detective Jacks said, "Sir, we need to speak to your wife. Is she home?"

Peter's ears turned red with frustration, but he kept his cool. Chloe appeared at his shoulder. Taking his hand, she asked, "What's going on, babe?"

Peter said, "Detectives. They want to talk to you."

Chloe asked the detectives, "Is someone hurt?"

Detective Jacks said, "Fortunately, no one is hurt, ma'am. There is a serious situation though. We need a statement from you."

Chloe bit her lip. She asked, "What happened?"

Sergeant Sanders said, "Puffs bakery has been burnt to the ground. You were fired yesterday, is that correct?"

Chloe squeezed Peter's hand. She said, "Yes. I was

fired."

Detective Jacks scribbled in his pad. He asked, "Do you know of anyone with a motive to rob and torch the bakery?"

Chloe began trembling. She asked, "Am I a suspect? I wouldn't do something like that."

Detective Jacks said, "It's an open investigation, ma'am."

Chloe said, "I didn't do it."

Sergeant Sanders said, "We have to cover all the bases, Mrs. Apple. We aren't accusing you of anything."

Chloe teared up and it drove Peter mad. He said, "You're upsetting my wife. Ask what you need to ask quickly or this conversation is over."

Detective Jacks asked, "Where were you at one o'clock this morning, ma'am?"

"I was asleep with my husband."

Both of the officers looked at Peter. Peter said, "She was here with me and I can assure you she's no burglar or arsonist. I've had enough of this so if she's not under arrest, I'm going to ask politely that you leave, please."

Detective Jacks scribbled away in his notepad, then closed it and put it in his pocket. Sergeant Sanders pulled a card out of his pocket and handed it to Chloe. He said, "If you hear anything or have anything else you want to talk to us about give us a call. Have a nice day folks."

The two men left the porch and headed towards their unmarked, silver police cruiser.

58

Rebecca showed up at the Apples' Sunday evening. Chloe greeted her excitedly—and nervously. Giving Rebecca a hug, she said, "I hope you're ready to meet my family. They're all anxious to know you."

Rebecca smiled. "I'm ready."

Chloe led her in by the hand. Mila and Barry were on the living room floor watching a comedy. They both looked up at the same time. Chloe said, "This is my friend. Come say hello."

Mila sprung from the floor and walked directly up to Rebecca. She said, "You're really pretty."

"Thank you, baby. So are you. Who's that handsome guy over there?"

Chloe turned red in the face instantly. Then she realized Rebecca was talking about Barry. Barry sauntered over. He asked, "What's your name?"

Rebecca knelt down. She said, "I'm Rebecca. Who are you?"

"I'm Barry. Will you be my girlfriend?"

Rebecca stood with a wide smile. She said, "Adorable. I don't think your momma wants you having a girlfriend yet."

Barry looked at Chloe with a question in his eyes. She said, "Get back to your show, honey. Rebecca and mommy are going to go have some adult time."

Barry frowned; he and Mila went back to the program. Chloe took Rebecca's hand and led her into the kitchen to meet Peter. He didn't seem to notice them in the doorway, while he busied himself preparing the meal.

Chloe cleared her throat. She said, "Babe, I want you to meet my friend."

Peter turned with batter on his hands from breading the fish. He said, "Hey, Rebecca, right?"

"That's me."

"Great. I've heard a lot about you. Very interesting."

"You know, I do try."

Chloe said, "How about a drink, Rebecca? I've got some red wine."

Rebecca said, "Sure. I could use a drink."

Chloe retrieved a bottle from the chiller. She put it on the counter and Peter washed his hands. He opened the bottle while Chloe took two glasses off the rack and handed one to Rebecca. Peter poured them both a glass. Chloe told Rebecca, "Follow me. The back porch is nice, if you like gardens."

The curious look sparkled in Rebecca's eyes. She said, "Beautiful. I'd like to see this garden."

Chloe led the way. Before they exited the back door, Peter said, "Don't have too much fun out there."

Rebecca laughed. She said, "I'll try to contain

myself."

Chloe led Rebecca to the cushioned patio furniture. She said, "Don't mind him. He's a big jokester."

"Oh, no, baby. Your family is adorable. Makes me jealous."

Chloe laughed. She said, "I doubt that. You're one of the most interesting people I've ever met. I don't think you'd want to give that up."

"I couldn't if I wanted. I can't have children."

"Well, I can't have any more, after Barry. There were complications. Couldn't you adopt?"

"I've never met anyone I liked enough to adopt a child with. Plus, you're right. I'm not ready to give up my lifestyle."

Chloe asked, "Did you hear about Puff's bakery?"

"Yeah. The police came knocking on my door early in the morning. I had to give alibies and shit. Pissed me off. I was so hung over, and I just got laid."

Chloe covered her mouth and feigned shock. She said, "Rebecca! You're so bad."

"Baby, you have no clue. Anyway, I could care less about the bakery getting robbed and torched. After the way Julissa treated you, I wanted to burn the place to the ground myself."

"Stop. You're just saying that."

"Baby, we're both looking for jobs now."

Taking a sip of her wine and looking at her friend, Chloe felt a sadness. She hadn't thought about Grace lately, but sitting outside with Rebecca made her relive her loss. Choking back tears, she could see Rebecca noticed something was wrong. Wiping her eyes, Chloe sat quietly.

Rebecca asked, "What's wrong? Did I say something?"

Chloe took a deep breath. She said, "No. It's not you at all. I started thinking about a friend I lost a couple of years ago."

Chloe hadn't seen concern on Rebecca's face until that point. She could see Rebecca cared for her deeply and it made Chloe feel loved. After a moment, Chloe told her new found friend the story that tore her heart to pieces.

59

Preparing the children for school Monday morning was a hectic task. Rushing to get them there on time, Chloe thought about the night before. She had confided in Rebecca and it made her feel pleased. Rebecca had listened and responded as if she cared for Grace, also. Chloe knew that wasn't the case, but she felt like Rebecca cared how it affected her.

Dropping Mila and Barry off at school, Chloe asked Mila, "Are you going to try to have a good day?"

Mila smiled. She said, "Yes, Mommy. I'm gonna have a good day."

Chloe said, "Don't let anyone get to you, baby. You're going to do great."

Barry stood next to Mila with a concerned look on his face. It was obvious he didn't want to go back to class. Chloe looked at him. She asked, "What's wrong, sweetie?"

Barry looked at the ground, then back at Chloe. He said, "Nobody likes me here."

Chloe said, "Honey, if you're nice, you'll make friends. You made friends with Steven."

"Yeah, I guess."

"You two run along. You're going to be late for class."

The children turned and walked towards the building. Chloe watched them in the sea of kids, until they disappeared inside the doorway. She started her car and drove away, praying that her babies have a good day.

60

Inside the school Mila's ears throbbed. Excited children filled the halls. She couldn't help feeling tense. Elvin Craig was nowhere in sight, but she knew she would be seeing him. The thought of being confronted by the boy made her nervous.

She asked Barry, "Do you think I can come stand with you after school, boo-boo?"

Barry had a puzzled look on his face. He said, "I don't care. You can if you want."

"Okay. I'll meet you."

The children separated. Mila felt miniscule in the hallway. She didn't want to talk to Sandra or Veronica, either. Stomach turning into knots, she entered her first class. The children were talking and running around the desks. Veronica sat in her seat smiling at Mila. Mila sat in the seat next to her.

Veronica asked, "What happened Friday?"

Mila said, "I had to leave. I felt sick."

"Are you sure it's not because of Elvin? Sandra said she told you we talked to him and you left class."

"I don't like him."

"We didn't know. We thought you did."

"Now he's going to harass me. Why would y'all tell him something like that?"

"We were just trying to be helpful. I promise. We weren't trying to embarrass you."

"Well, that's the way I felt. I don't even want to be here now."

"It'll be okay, Mila. He probably doesn't even care. He acted like he didn't."

Mila felt a hot flush and knew her face was turning red. She said, "I don't want to talk about it. I just want it to go away."

"Don't worry. We'll tell him you don't like him. He'll leave you alone."

"No! Don't say anything to him about me. It's bad enough already."

Veronica frowned. She said, "Okay. I'm sorry."

The teacher walked in and the class settled down. Mila's mind churned in high speed. She wanted to leave. Going home wasn't an option this time. Calming herself, she focused on the teacher and tried her best not to think about Elvin Craig.

CHAPTER 61

Barry Apple *was not* enjoying class. All the children avoided him like a flesh eating virus. Ironically, the only child that would come near him was the same child he had assaulted. Steven and Barry were the odd kids and although skittish, Steven sat next to Barry. He asked, "Do you want to eat lunch with me? My mom packed you a pudding pack."

Barry felt relieved, happy that Steven had forgiven him. At lunch time Barry sat across from him and they ate the meals that their mothers had packed them. Steven passed Barry a chocolate pudding cup. He said, "My mom says you can come over whenever you want. I don't have any friends."

Barry took the pudding and thought it seemed like he was being bribed. He said, "You don't have to give me things to be my friend."

A kid passed close to the table and Steven jerked around to see who it was, then looked at Barry. He said, "I get nervous around people."

Barry said, "It's okay. You don't have to be nervous. I won't let anyone hurt you."

Steven smiled. Opening his pudding, he said, "Then we are friends."

62

Mila watched the clock, waiting for the day to be over. The hours crept by as slowly as an ant troop carrying away a beetle carcass. She felt sick inside. It wasn't hard for her to imagine herself being that carcass. All her fellow students, dragging her away to be devoured. The thought made her shiver.

The dismissal bell rang and relief washed over her. The day had gone by without complication, all she had to do now was brace herself for the school yard and make it to her mother's car. The other students flooded out of the room and Mila took her time putting her books away. Sandra stayed in the room, waiting on Mila.

Mila said, "Go ahead. I'm going to wait with my brother today."

Sandra asked, "Is this about that boy?"

"No. Not really."

"Okay. Veronica and I saw him at lunch. You don't have to worry about him. We told him to leave you alone, that you didn't like him."

The hairs on Mila's arms stood up. She felt the knots

return to her stomach. The kind of sick feeling rose in her that made her want to vomit all over her friend. Mila asked, "Why would you do that? I told Veronica to leave it alone. Didn't she tell you?"

Sandra said, "She said something. I just thought it was the right thing to do."

Mila said, "Well, it wasn't. Jeez. You're ruining my life."

Sandra looked shocked. She said, "We're not trying to ruin your life, Mila. We're trying to help."

"Stop already. Just leave it alone. Leave me alone."

Picking up her backpack, Mila left the room frustrated to the point that tears threatened to spill. The hallway was still packed with students at the lockers, but there was a current flowing out the doors. Mila dropped her head low, praying she could make it out without having to talk to anyone. She didn't want to see Veronica, and the last person she wanted to see would be Elvin.

Exhilarated to make it through the exit without being confronted by anyone, she squinted in the daylight. The warmth of the sun on her skin felt energizing. Looking around for Barry's class, she couldn't spot them anywhere. Spotting Elvin across the yard made her skin crawl. He was looking at her with an evil smirk.

Barry appeared at her side. He said, "What are you looking at, sissy?"

Mila looked at him and smiled. "Nothing, boo-boo. I'm ready to go home though. How was your day?"

"It was good. I didn't get in any trouble."

"That's good. Mommy and daddy are going to be proud."

A hand clutched Mila's arm. She spun around, there stood Elvin Craig. He said, "Tell your snot nose friends to leave me alone."

Mila said, "I didn't tell them to talk to you. They just did."

Elvin squeezed Mila's arm harder. He said, "I'm not above kickin' a girl's butt."

Mila said, "Let go of my arm. You're hurting me."

Outraged, Barry yelled. "Let go of my sister!"

He ran towards Elvin, swinging his arms. Elvin let go of Mila and pushed Barry to the ground. Standing close by, Mrs. Marsh noticed the disturbance. Students gathered around. She waded through the crowd, before Barry could get off the ground. She said, "Both of you. To the principal's office." After calling on her radio, it wasn't long before two other teachers came to escort them.

63

Chloe sat in the office with Principal Walker and Mrs. Marsh. Principal Walker said, "I am appalled that Barry's first day back ended in a fight. Principal Walker is supposed to believe that Barry is some kind of innocent in all of this? I think not. Fighting is fighting. Barry is going to be in detention for the next three days. If he gets into any more fights it will be permanent suspension for this school year. You've plead your case and I have spoken."

Chloe's frustration ate at her conscience. She wanted to give the principal a tongue lashing, but she knew it would make the situation worse. Standing, Chloe gathered her things. She said, "If we're done here, I'll be leaving now."

Principal Walker said, "I suppose we are. I warned you that this type of behavior won't be tolerated. Principal Walker must have order."

Chloe wanted to rip the woman's hair out. She left the office in a fury. Mila and Barry sat in the little wooden chairs outside the office along with Elvin Craig and his mother. Elvin's mother was not the friendly type. Scowling at Chloe like the situation was her fault and patting her son's strawberry red head. The woman said, "You keep those two brats in check. They better not be bothering my boy again."

Chloe didn't respond to the belligerent woman. She left the office with Barry and Mila in tow, glad to be leaving the school. In the car the mood was static. There wasn't a peep coming from the back seat. Chloe adjusted the rearview and looked at Barry. He sat with a grimace on his face, staring out the window. Chloe asked, "Are you okay, sweetie?"

Barry didn't respond. He shifted in his booster seat, but didn't take his attention from the window. Chloe looked at Mila. She asked, "Are you okay?"

Mila said, "I really don't want to go to school anymore."

Chloe bit her lip. She said, "Sweetie, you have to go to school."

Mila said, "You could homeschool us, Mommy. You don't have a job. I don't like this place anymore."

Chloe started the car. She sat for a moment, thinking. She said, "We have to talk to your daddy about all of this. I don't know if I can do homeschool."

Putting the car in drive, Chloe pulled away from Clinton Elementary.

64

Barry wore a grimace at the dinner table that night. Images of the older boy grabbing Mila and pushing him to the ground kept playing over in his mind. He felt infuriated. Chloe kept trying to talk to him but it didn't help. He didn't want to talk about it. Being good was no longer on his mind. Wishing he could kill the boy, he dreamed of ways to hurt the red-headed menace.

Chloe asked, "Is everything okay, Barry? You're not touching your chicken or potatoes."

Poking his chicken with his fork, he wondered if the fork would kill the boy. The thought of the utensil piercing the boy's retina made him smile. He poked the chicken again and imagined the kind of painful scream that would issue from the bully's throat.

Peter said, "That's a wicked looking smile you've got, son. What's on your mind?"

Barry looked at Peter and the smile faded. He said, "I'm not hungry."

"Your mother made all of this for you and you don't want to eat? Fried chicken is one of your favorites."

"I know. I'm just not hungry."

"Okay, go get washed up. Bedtime, soon."

Barry left the table. He went to the bathroom and washed his hands and face. Brushing his teeth in the mirror, he thought about the glass. Wondering where he could get some glass to cut the boy, his thoughts wandered to the knives in the kitchen. There were so many weapons. His thoughts festered with hatred.

That night, lying in bed, a movie came to Barry's mind. In the movie he saw guys putting items in socks to beat someone with. He thought about the scene, then he climbed out of bed and looked at his socks. They were too small, he thought. Deciding to get one of his father's socks, he snuck into his parents' bathroom. He found a long, white sock and went back to his room. Sitting on his bed he wondered what to put in it. A warm feeling rose inside him when the idea to put rocks in the sock came to him. Wanting to laugh, he stopped himself. Waking anyone might ruin his deviant plan.

The night was thick with darkness when he stepped onto the back porch. His mother had rocks in her garden and Barry was on a mission. Finding several to do the damage, Barry went to the tree in the yard. Wanting to test the weapon, he reached back with the rock sling and struck the tree. Bark flew, and the thud was loud enough to give him a scare. The last thing he wanted was to be discovered. Hurrying inside, he hid the weapon in his backpack and laid down with a grin that didn't go away until he was fast asleep.

65

Getting ready for school, Barry smiled and ate his cereal. Chloe said, "It looks like you're feeling better this morning, mister. Are you ready to have a good day?"

"Oh, yeah. Today is going to rock." Thinking of his little inside joke made him smile even wider.

Mila said, "I'm depressed. I don't want to go. I don't know what boo-boo's so happy about, I'm miserable."

Chloe said, "Sweetie, that attitude is making you miserable. You have to *think* happy to *be* happy."

"I'm not thinking happy, Mommy. It's gonna be horrible. I know."

Barry thought, *'Yeah, it's going to be horrible for someone. I'm going to let that butthead have it. I'll teach him about messing with me. He's not touching my sister again. I'll kill him.'*

Chloe said, "It's getting late. We have to load up and get to school."

Chloe smoothed Mila's hair. Mila smiled. Chloe said, "Everything's going to be okay, honey."

The radio played quietly in the car. Barry felt anxious. He also felt proud of himself for creating the weapon. Thinking of leveling the bigger boy brought him pleasure.

Pulling up to the school, Chloe said, "Okay. You two have a good day. Try not to get into any trouble."

Mila exited and Barry let himself out of his booster seat. He climbed out of the car. Stepping onto the school's lawn he felt energized. Mila waited to walk him to class. He walked with her for a moment, then looked back to see if his mother had pulled away yet. Seeing she was gone, he stopped.

Mila said, "Come on, boo-boo. We have to go to class."

Barry said, "I know my way."

"I'm supposed to make sure you get there safe."

Barry furrowed his brow. He said, "I'm not a baby."

"I know, boo-boo. It's not that, really."

"I want to walk alone."

"Why are you being like this? The bell's gonna ring soon."

"Don't be a stupid-head. Leave me alone."

"Okay, be that way." Mila stuck her tongue out and walked away.

Knowing he didn't have much time, Barry went in behind Mila and began scanning the halls for Elvin Craig.

66

Elvin's red hair was like a beacon shining from midway down the East hall. Barry watched him lean against a locker talking to a girl. Putting his backpack down, Barry pulled the rock sling out, wrapped it in his hand, and stalked towards Elvin with malicious intent. Once within range, he reared back.

Elvin noticed Barry a second too late. His eyes were golf balls upon impact. The blow landed solidly against his jaw with a loud crack. Elvin's head hit the locker and he crumpled. A scream from the girl he had been talking to alerted everyone in the hallway who hadn't witnessed the brutality.

Blood spilled from Elvin's mouth in a pool of liquid aftermath. Barry spat on the unconscious bully. He said, "Don't ever touch my sister."

Dropping the sock, Barry began walking away; then, a teacher grabbed him. Fighting the teacher's grip in a fury, Barry started yelling profanities. "Fuck you! Fuck all of you!"

Another teacher grabbed him and the two pinned him to the ground. One of the teachers said, "Someone run and get the principal! Tell her there's a student hurt badly. Call 911."

Groups of children ran to be the messenger as the bell rang out for class.

67

Chloe sat across from Principal Walker, gritting her teeth while the woman talked. Principal Walker said, "I knew he was going to pull something. This will not be tolerated. Nothing like this has happened on Principal Walker's watch in all the years. Your son is a deviant and he will no longer be welcome on this campus. He belongs in a reformatory! He was seen taking another pudding from poor Steven Whitaker yesterday, and now this. He broke a student's jaw! This will not be tolerated."

Officer Raymond Tinsel sat with his arms crossed. Beady eyes trained on Chloe. She wanted to tell him how stupid his large ears looked on his tiny head. His stare wore at her nerves like a wool pad scraping against the silk that was her patience for the duo. Frustration boiled in her gut.

Unable to hold her tongue any longer, her frustrations from past visits with Principal Walker boiled over and spilled out like crude oil bursting through the ground. Chloe said, "You're a pompous woman. I can't stand to hear you speak."

Principal Walker's eyes opened wide, startled. Chloe continued, "Barry may be a deviant, but he's my deviant. I don't think I can tolerate hearing you talk about him anymore. As a matter of fact, I don't want to hear you talk at all. I'm pulling both of my children out of your precious school. If you refer to yourself in third person one more time in my presence, I think I'll vomit."

Principal Walker huffed. She said, "I'm not sure I've ever met anyone quite as rude as you, Mrs. Apple. I may be getting a clear vision of why— "

"Don't you say it, bitch." Chloe stood and gave the principle an obscene gesture with her middle finger. "I'll be leaving now."

She turned on her heel and stalked out. Principal Walker clucked in disapproval. Chloe shut the office door behind herself and looked at the school secretary. Leeann looked her usual perky self. The red head didn't give the slightest hint in her green eyes that she'd heard the conversation from the office. Chloe thought that maybe she hadn't.

Chloe asked, "Where's my son?"

Leeann said, "He's with Trisha, the school counselor. You've met her, right? I can take you to her if you want."

The woman's energy disturbed Chloe. Chloe said, "I know where her office is. Is she there?"

"Oh, yes!" Leeann scurried from around her desk. She said, "Come on. I'll walk with you."

Chloe left the office with the bubbly woman. When

they were a few feet down the hall, Leeann turned her head to speak to Chloe. She said, "You're my new hero."

Puzzled by the comment, Chloe didn't respond. Leeann said, "The way you told that witch off. It was amazing."

"I didn't know you could hear us."

"Oh, yeah. I hear everything."

The thought made Chloe uneasy. When they reached the counselor's door, Leeann said, "I'm not going in. Good luck." She turned and walked away.

Chloe entered the counselor's office, not knowing what to expect. What she saw surprised her. Barry had a toy car, sitting next to Trisha on the floor. She was playing Hot Wheels with him. Barry wore a smile, and so did the counselor. They both paused and looked at her.

Trisha said, "Come in, Mrs. Apple." Her inviting smile made Chloe feel comfortable.

Chloe walked in and closed the door behind herself. She said, "I'm going to be leaving with Barry now. We won't be back."

Trisha stood. She said, "It's a shame that things have gone the way they have. What did Principal Walker say?"

"It doesn't matter. Barry won't be attending Clinton anymore and neither will his sister."

"It's really a shame. I presume you'll be enrolling them in another school in the district?"

"I'm thinking about homeschool."

"That could be good, or bad. Social skills are important."

"I know. Right now, I think it's the best thing."

Talking about homeschool made Chloe think about how she would have no time to herself. The counselor's remark brought to mind Mila having friends. She didn't want her children to be social outcasts. It felt disturbing to think of either of them with no friends. Chloe said, "I'm going to need to pull Mila out of class. I'll figure out exactly what to do later. For now, my children are coming with me."

68

Barry hadn't talked to Chloe about what happened. The day went by slowly for her, she hadn't called Peter to let him know she pulled the children out of school. She wanted to tell him in person and discuss it. Praying he would be understanding, she prepared pork chops for dinner and tried to quiet her mind.

When Peter arrived, the children ran to greet him in the foyer. Before the kids released their grips on his leg and waist, Chloe walked up and kissed Peter. He smiled and patted Barry on the head. He said, "I always love this greeting. I wish these rug rats would stay this size forever."

Chloe said, "I fried pork chops."

"It smells delicious, and I'm starved. Let me jump in the shower and I'm ready to devour."

Chloe laughed and rolled her eyes. Touching Peter's arm, she said, "You're such a cheese, babe."

"You love it."

The children released him and he headed towards the back of the house. Mila asked, "Are you going to tell him about today, Mommy?"

"I'll tell him at dinner, sweetie. We can all talk about it together."

69

Dinner served, Peter took a bite of his pork chop and swallowed. He said, "Sugar plum, you outdid yourself. This is the best pork chop I ever had."

Mila giggled. Chloe said, "Flattery. I can deal with that. Are you buttering me up for something?"

"I'm serious. This is awesome. There is something I wanted to talk to you about, though."

Chloe grinned. "Okay. You go first, because I have something to tell you, also."

"Well, my buddy from work, Jordan Roberts. Do you remember him?"

"The chain smoker with a limp, real country?"

"Yeah. Him. He has a '55 Chevy Belair he'll sell me for dirt cheap. It's solid and has a killer motor in it. I'd like to get it."

At this point Chloe would normally put up an argument about saving and a barrage of other concerns, she resisted the urge to begin pointing out negatives. She said, "If we can afford it, I don't see why not."

Peter looked confused. No doubt he had cooked up rebuttals, endless counter arguments, on his way home from work. His look of confusion changed to concern. He said, "That's too easy, sugar. What the heck do you have going on in that sweet mind of yours?"

Chloe bit her lip. She looked from Barry to Mila. Both children focused on their plates like they were oblivious to the conversation. Chloe said, "I pulled the kids out of school today."

Peter showed no signs of agitation. He asked, "Are they gonna go back tomorrow?"

"No. I pulled them out for good."

Peter shifted in his seat and looked from Chloe to the children and back. He asked, "So, what's the plan?"

"I'm going to homeschool them."

Peter raised his eyebrows. "Do you really want to do that?"

"Yes. I think it's the best thing at this point."

"That bad, huh? What happened?"

Chloe told Peter the day's events. Sitting quietly for a moment, he ran his fingers through his hair. He said, "You're going to have a lot on your plate, sugar."

"I know. I'm prepared."

Barry and Mila smiled at one another and the family finished their meal. An underlying tension filled the air.

70

Chloe woke and felt burdened. She knew she had paperwork to do and people to call. Peter was getting ready for work. Watching him pull on his pants, she had an overwhelming urge to ask him a question. A question that she wasn't sure she should ask, but necessary.

She asked, "Do you support me in my decision about the kids?"

Peter took a deep breath. He sat on the edge of the bed and ran his fingers through his hair. After what seemed like an excruciatingly long pause to her, he said, "I think we should have talked about it first, Chloe. It's a big decision. When I get home we'll need to talk about other options rather than homeschooling."

A sick chill ran up Chloe's spine. It was rare Peter called her by her actual name. She felt his frustration in the words he spoke. All she wanted was to make it right. Having Peter on her team meant everything to her. Acting rashly, she had made the call to pull the children out, and now she regretted it. Barry wouldn't have been able to return, but Mila was the subject.

Taking her out without talking to Peter wasn't the best solution. Even if they would have seen things on the same level, she had taken away his vote as Mila's father.

Chloe said, "Babe, I didn't want to deal with that bitch principal anymore. Please don't hate me."

"Sugar, why are you acting crazy? I wouldn't hate you no matter what you did. I don't have to be happy about what you do, either. Right now, I've got to get to work. I'm not trying to argue."

"You know I don't like it when you call me crazy. You never call me that anymore."

"Chloe, please, let's do this tonight."

Peter put his work cap on and walked out the door. With the conflict unresolved, Chloe wasn't going to be able to stop thinking about the small argument. She wished she hadn't asked the question. Thinking about how when they were kids Peter used to tease her about being impulsive and crazy, she smashed her face into one of the pillows on the bed and screamed.

71

Barry and Mila sat at the kitchen table wondering why their mother wasn't making breakfast. Peter barely kissed them before storming out the door. Mila had a tendency to think that when her parents argued, or anything went wrong, that she was somehow at fault. Even when it wasn't her fault and she knew it by logic, she still thought she should do something in almost every situation to make things better.

Mila asked Barry, "Do you want cereal, boo-boo? I can get it."

"Okay."

Mila went to the cupboard and pulled out two boxes. She placed them on the table, then set out to gather bowls, utensils and milk. The children ate in silence. Mila heard her mother's bedroom door open and she perked up. Chloe walked into the kitchen in her bath robe.

Mila said, "Good morning, Mommy!"

Chloe looked at her. She said, "I don't know what's so good about it."

Mila smiled. "We're going to spend the day together.

Isn't that good?"

Chloe cocked her head to the side. "You know what, sweetie. It is good. What do you want to do?"

"Could we go to the park and have a picnic?"

"Sure, honey. We can do that."

Barry groaned. Chloe said, "I don't want to hear anything out of you, mister. All the trouble you caused, you better be happy to go to the park with us."

"Momma, I just wanna play. I don't care where we're at."

"Enjoy. Because there's going to be work ahead."

Mila felt content. Her mother didn't seem too upset now, and that made her happy.

72

Chloe was preparing a basket for the picnic when her phone rang. She looked at the caller ID and could see it was Rebecca calling. She answered and her friend's seductive voice came into the earpiece before Chloe could get a word out. Rebecca said, "Baby, tell me you have time for me today."

"I'm going on a picnic with the children."

"Beautiful. I'll tag along. I need a friend."

Chloe didn't want to turn her away. She said, "Okay. No smoking and no cursing."

Rebecca laughed. "How dare you. I would never."

Chloe smiled. "Come over and you can ride with us."

"I'll be there in ten."

Chloe hung up and called Mila into the kitchen. Chloe asked, "How do you feel about Rebecca coming to the park with us?"

"Are you kidding? We love Aunt Rebecca!"

Chloe was taken back. Since when did they start calling her aunt Rebecca? Chloe said, "That's good. Go tell your brother to get ready. We'll be leaving shortly."

Mila ran to tell Barry the news. Soon there was a knock, then someone entering the door. Chloe went around the foyer and found Rebecca there. Rebecca walked up and hugged Chloe. She said, "I've missed you. Why haven't you called me?"

Chloe shook her head. She said, "It's been crazy. You wouldn't believe everything that happened in the last couple of days."

"I wish I would have known. You can call me about anything. You know that, right?"

"I know. I just don't like bothering people about every little thing."

"Sounds like there's been some big things. We're family, you call me."

"About that. Did you know Mila calls you Aunt Rebecca?"

"I know. I hope you don't mind. I told her she could call me that. She asked and I didn't want to tell her she couldn't."

"When did you tell her that?"

Rebecca had her signature curious look. She said, "I gave her my number in case of emergencies the other night at dinner."

"Why would you do that?"

"Well. You told me how she almost walked out of school the other day. I was worried she would wander off and not know who to call. So I had a little conversation with her."

Chloe said, "You two are so sneaky, I swear. I should be pissed."

"Are you?"

The children ran from around the corner and wrapped themselves around the guest, obviously having listened to the whole conversation. Chloe rolled her eyes. She said, "I'll get over it."

73

The day was sunny but windblown; the park empty of any other occupants. They set their pallet close to the playground and Chloe opened the basket. She passed out plastic cups and poured everyone orange juice. Rebecca and the children were all smiling. It was infectious to Chloe; she couldn't help the smile that spread on her face.

Rebecca said, "This is a nice park. Too bad all the other children are in school, you guys have no one to play with."

Mila said, "I don't mind. I have you, mommy and Barry. That's all I care about right now."

Barry asked, "Will you push me on the swing, Aunt Rebecca?"

Rebecca looked at Chloe with question in her expression. Chloe told Barry, "You have to eat a sandwich and some chips first, then you can go on the playground."

"Okay."

"I don't know if Rebecca wants to push you, either."

Rebecca said, "I'll push him. As long as he's not a

scaredy baby."

Barry said, "I'm not a scaredy. I like going high."

"Beautiful. I'll push you then."

Mila giggled and Chloe began passing out sandwiches and little Ziploc bags with servings of chips.

74

Rebecca pushed the swing as hard and high as she could. She was curious what went on in such a seemingly innocent, but devious child's mind such as Barry's. He laughed and cried out to be pushed higher and faster. It was an intriguing thing to Rebecca, the mind of a child. She wondered how much of what Barry did was premeditated. It was obvious the attacks at school were. In Rebecca's world there were monsters of all kinds and they fascinated her.

Rebecca said, "That's enough for now."

She looked over at Mila and Chloe. They were talking to each other, oblivious to her and Barry. Rebecca left the playground and sat at the bench next to it. The one that parents sit at to watch their children play. Wondering what it would be like to actually be a parent, she watched Barry's swing slow and then him jumping out into the wood chips that made up the playground floor.

Barry ran over to Rebecca and sat next to her. He sat close and snugged up. Reaching out, Barry took her hand. He said, "I like you. You're real pretty and fun."

Rebecca said, "Baby, that's what all the guys say. Are you trying to butter me up?"

"What's that mean?"

"Beautiful. Can I ask you a question?"

"I don't care."

"Okay. What was going through your head when you hit that kid at school?"

"Which one?"

"Oh yeah, multiple assaults. When you hit the boy yesterday. Let's start there."

"I had to do it. He wasn't going to stop picking on my sister."

"What about when he pushed you down?"

"That, too."

"No, I mean what were you thinking?"

"I wished I was bigger so I could kick his butt."

"What made you think of using a weapon?"

"How else could I do it?"

"I guess you have a point."

75

Chloe looked at Barry and Rebecca sitting on the bench hand in hand. A pang of jealousy rose in her stomach. Barry never held her hand. Although he had become much sweeter in the passing week, he rarely showed affection. There was something about Rebecca that the children liked and it drove Chloe a little mad. She could understand to a degree; Rebecca was a likable person.

Chloe told Mila, "Go see what Rebecca and Barry are doing over there. Ask them to join us."

Mila ran across the lawn to where they were sitting and Chloe watched her interact with them. Barry and Rebecca stood and both children took her hands. They walked back towards Chloe. She admired the way Rebecca's sun dress looked. The children looked happy with her, but Rebecca didn't look the part of a mother. Chloe thought she looked attractive and somehow single and available without a care.

When the group sat next to her, she asked, "How do you do it Rebecca? How do you make everyone fall in love with you?"

"I know. I'm not sure. Not everyone falls in love with me, though. I don't have many friends."

Chloe felt terrible for her jealous feelings. She hoped it didn't show. Loving Rebecca wasn't the worst thing that could happen. After all the horrible things that had happened in the last few weeks, years even, it should be a relief to find someone like her. Feeling pleased that the ugly turn of her stomach had gone, Chloe smiled and resolved to enjoy the afternoon.

76

Smiling when the buzzer sounded that signaled the end of his shift, Peter put his tools up and retrieved his lunch box from his locker. Jordan walked with him towards the parking lot. They talked about the classic car Peter wanted to buy from him. Excitement filled Peter's thoughts.

Jordan said, "You can make payments if you want. I don't mind."

Peter said, "I'm gonna get the cash, don't worry about it. Probably do it this weekend. I've got some things goin' on with the family I have to straighten out, then I can take care of it."

They pushed through the double doors that led into the parking lot. There was a large man standing beside the doors. He pushed away from the wall and stumbled. When he spoke he slurred and reeked of alcohol.

He asked, "Is one of you Peter Apple?"

Peter looked at Jordan puzzled, then back to the man. "I'm Peter."

The man said, "I'm Elvin Craig Senior, and your son broke my son's jaw."

"I'm sorry about that, but what are you doing at my work?"

"I'm here to break your jaw."

The man lunged forward, swinging wide. Peter deflected the punch and countered with a stiff right hook, out of reflex. The man dropped to the ground like a fallen store mannequin, stiffly and quietly, he was down for the count. Peter knelt and so did Jordan. They both observed that the drunk was breathing.

Jordan said, "Maybe you should get out of here. Won't do much good to be around when he wakes up."

"I don't know if that's a good idea."

"Man, he was looking for a fight and he found it. If anyone comes out, I'll tell them he's some drunk passed out on the property. You could lose your job for fighting in the lot. Your fault or not. Just go on home, I'll take care of this."

Reluctantly, Peter left Jordan with the unconscious man and headed for his truck. Leaving the parking lot, he could see several other people gathering around where Elvin Craig Sr. lay. Peter stepped on the gas and left the trouble behind. He felt queasy. There was no doubt in his mind that there would be some type of repercussion.

77

Chloe turned the boiling water off. The noodles were perfect and the spaghetti sauce tasted magnificent. She pulled the garlic bread from the oven and placed it in a large decorative bowl to cool. Everything needed to be perfect in her mind. Preparing the meal with care, she hoped it would calm Peter's nerves. It always made her feel special when she knew that her husband enjoyed his meal; furthermore, it could help with the minor spat. At least she prayed it would.

Peter walked in and the kids ran to meet him in the foyer. Chloe turned the corner smiling, but her smile became a frown of puzzlement when she saw Peter's demeanor. Cold eyes in a stony face, he was obviously disturbed. Chloe immediately thought his mood was her fault. He hugged the children, and headed straight to the master bedroom without uttering a word. Something about the distant look in his eyes alarmed Chloe to the point that she wasn't sure if she should go after him.

Chloe told the children, "Go watch your show, babies. We'll have dinner shortly."

The children walked away with looks of concern. They had apparently read the same silent message in their daddy's demeanor. Panic began to rise within Chloe and formed a sour lump in her throat. She didn't want to lose Peter. Thinking she had to make amends, and quickly, she rushed back to the room. When she entered she could hear the shower running. Peter's clothes were scattered across the floor and the bathroom door was cracked open. She gingerly walked to the door and knocked. He didn't answer. She went into the bathroom and sat on the toilet lid.

Chloe said, "Babe, I don't want you to be mad at me anymore."

Peter turned the shower off. There was a chasm of silence. Chloe said, "I'll do anything. Just tell me what to do."

Peter said, "It smells delicious in there. Big meal?"

"I cooked spaghetti and meat sauce, just the way you like it. Extra buttery garlic bread and everything."

Peter stepped out of the shower and began toweling himself dry. Chloe asked, "Are you going to stay mad at me?"

"Sugar plum, I was over that by lunch, you know I can't stay mad at you."

"Then why are you acting strange?"

Peter shook his head and ran his fingers through his hair. He said, "I don't want to talk about it now, sugar." He tossed the towel over her head playfully.

Chloe threw the cloth to the floor. She said, "When? Is it that bad?"

"I just don't want to worry you or ruin your appetite. Please, sugar, let's talk about it after dinner, when the kids are in bed."

"Okay. Promise you'll tell me."

"I will. I promise."

"Okay. I'll let you get dressed and we can eat." She frowned.

Peter asked, "What's wrong now? Everything's fine, baby."

"I'm worried."

"Don't be, it's probably nothing."

"I can't help but worry. I saw how much whatever it is bothered you."

"Oh, it still bothers me, but it's gonna be fine." He leaned down and kissed her forehead.

He said, "Please, babe, after dinner."

"Okay, mister, but I don't like it already."

78

During dinner Peter occasionally stared into space, shaken by the hatred that Elvin Craig had shown toward him. Anxiety settled in his chest and restricted his lungs. It had been a long time since he'd engaged in violence. The situation left him feeling awkward. If he could take back striking the man, he would. He had acted on reflex and the result was unsatisfactory for him.

He could see the concern on Chloe's face whenever she observed his distance. Experiencing the rotten feeling inside made him wish he could conceal the incident from Chloe. It was too late for that; she had noticed, and he couldn't have her believing his mood was her fault. Finishing his meal, he excused himself from the table.

In the bedroom he sat and went over the situation again, trying to figure out how to tell Chloe without causing too much alarm. He couldn't seem to find an easy way to put it. His mind conjured up images: The twisted look on the man's face, the blow he'd issued to his drunken adversary—the jarring images were ingrained on the template of his memory.

Chloe entered the room later in the evening. She said, "I've been trying to give you space. I know something is bothering you pretty bad, but it's time to say goodnight to the kids. Are you up for that?"

"Sure, sugar, I'll be there in a minute."

Chloe left the room and Peter took a deep breath. He didn't want his negative thoughts and feelings to transfer to the kids before they closed their eyes to sleep. Stilling himself, he thought of some of his favorite moments. The day he married Chloe. Bringing Mila home for the first time. Their excitement when they found out they were having another child. Once he felt serene, he went to put the children to bed.

79

Lying in bed, Chloe stared at Peter. She couldn't believe what she had just heard. There was a numb feeling inside her. It was just that type of feeling she was prone to having whenever she had no clue what to say. She was glad Peter hadn't been hurt. The thought of him leaving the man on the ground without a solid clue that he was okay didn't process well with her.

Of all the thoughts going through her mind, one stood out most. If the man knew where Peter worked, did he also know where they lived? Were they safe? Trying not to react on the thoughts and say something that might disturb Peter worse than he already was, she felt sick. Helpless. Adrift. Worried.

Draping her arm over the man she loved, she said the only thing that came naturally. "Everything's going to be okay, babe."

Peter rolled and embraced her. Before long they were both asleep, drained from stress.

80

Peter readied himself for work then sat at the breakfast table with Chloe and the children. He felt grateful to have them all in his life. Watching Chloe serve them and seeing the early morning smile on Mila's face lightened his heart. A good night's sleep had done well for him. His stress seemed to have melted away during the night hours.

The ride to work gave him some time to think again, alone. He wondered what Jordan would have to say about the previous day, he was curious to find out if the man had been belligerent when he'd revived. Imagining how the scene might have gone brought back the tight feeling in his chest. He decided to try calling Jordan.

Jordan answered. Peter asked, "How did things go yesterday? You know, with that guy."

Jordan said, "Man, I was going to call you yesterday, but I figured you'd call and it got late. I figured I'd see you at work."

"Yeah, well, I'm on my way. I guess I've been dreading it so I didn't want to talk much yesterday."

"Don't worry about it man. He woke up and I

helped him to his feet. The guy was so drunk I'm not sure he even realized what had happened when he woke up. Fuckin' loser, man. What kind of asshole gets drunk and starts a fight at another guy's work? Piece of shit."

"Yeah, I know. It's got me kind of worried. No tellin' what a jerk like that'll do."

"I wouldn't worry about it much. Fuckin' bastard is a fuckin' drunk. After that hook you threw, if he remembers, he won't be back."

"Let's hope so. I'll be there in a few minutes."

"Alright, man. I'll see you. We still doin' the car thing?"

"Yeah, this weekend."

"Good deal."

81

The road noise was hypnotic to Peter on the ride home. Wanting to believe it was over between him and Elvin Craig Sr., he thought that maybe Jordan was right. Maybe the unruly man had gotten enough? His jaw had to hurt, and the way he hit the ground must have left a few bruises.

Pulling up to the front of his house, he didn't want to go in showing his concern. He decided he'd had enough of worrying. Taking a deep breath, he exited the vehicle and headed for the front door with a smile. Wondering what kind of hell the children had put Chloe through while he was gone, he opened the door with a fixed smile, ready to interact.

By the time he was halfway inside, the children and Chloe were turning the corner to greet him. They were likely waiting all day to see him, considering his disposition of the day before. In that moment he reminded himself how fortunate he was to have them in his life. In the same moment, a loud pop seemed to echo through the sky and Peter's chest exploded.

It registered, as he looked at his family's blood

splattered faces, that he'd been shot. Their smiles turned to frowns and twisted expressions of terror as he fell to the floor. His life wasn't flashing before his eyes, his mind was filled only with the confrontation with Elvin Craig Sr. and the sound of Mila's scream. Peter took his last breath without being able to comprehend his family's hands on him, trying to pull him out of the open doorway into the house.

82

Chloe pulled as hard as she could, but she couldn't budge Peter in her panic, she was barely aware that blood had closed one of her eyes and that even the children were trying to help move his body. Blood pooled underneath him and spread outward, rendering the floor slippery, making it impossible to get good traction to aid their efforts. Another boom issued and the mirror in the foyer shattered with a violent burst.

The chaos pushed Chloe into survival mode, fearing for the safety of the children. Knowing Peter would want her to get the children to safety if he could speak, she grabbed Mila and Barry each by the arm. They were so consumed with grief and fear they didn't seem to notice the second gunshot. Pulling them away from their father, Chloe yelled, "We have to go! We have to get out of the doorway! Let go of your daddy!"

Mila cried out. "He's hurt, Mommy. We have to do something!"

"We can't help your daddy right now, baby. We have to get to safety and get help. That's what your daddy would want."

Chloe began dragging the children away. She felt a sickness inside, leaving Peter behind. Knowing she was doing the right thing, she pressed on. Dragging the children kicking and screaming, she looked out the back door's window. It looked clear and she didn't think there would be two shooters, but paranoia ate at her. She wondered if whoever shot Peter would come around the back to intercept them. The fear of staying in the house and the shooter coming in overtook Chloe as her thoughts turned to the neighbors. She didn't want to go to the next door neighbors because the villain might see her pushing the children over the fence on either side.

The children suddenly stopped moving and everything became eerily quiet. Mila sniffled. She said, "Mommy, we can't leave daddy."

"Sweetie. I don't want to. We have to. We have to make it across the alley and over one of the neighbor's fences. We can call an ambulance and the police from there."

Chloe took her hand off Mila and opened the door with a fear that Mila would run back to her father. When she stayed put, Chloe felt relieved. She said, "Both of you hold my hands tight. We're going to run across the yard and out the back gate."

Chloe gripped the children's small hands and left the home and Peter behind them. Mila was shaking and crying when they reached the neighbor's eight-foot wooden privacy fence, directly behind their property. Chloe didn't bother looking for a gate. She pushed

Barry over the top and heard him land on the other side of the fence with a thud.

She told Mila, "You next, baby. You've got to get over this fence."

Mila shuddered and cooperated with reluctance. When Mila was halfway over, a car turned into the alley. Chloe went into another panic. She pushed Mila over quickly and ran back across the pavement towards her gate. The car's engine revved and she could hear it speeding down the drive. By the time she reached the gate she heard the tires of the vehicle come to a loud screeching stop.

She ran for the house, expecting a bullet in the back at any moment. When she made it inside, she turned to close and lock the door, but the man was too close and approaching fast. Turning to run, she wanted to reach the closet and Peter's .38 revolver. Scrambling around the corner and into the hallway, she heard the man yell for her to stop. Panic propelled her to the bedroom and the pistol. Pulling the shoe box out the top of the closet, she found the weapon, but by the time she turned and raised it the man stood in the doorway.

Chloe didn't think, she squeezed the trigger three times and watched the man stumble back and fall to the ground, clutching his chest and stomach, he curled up and Chloe blacked out

83

Chloe woke on a stretcher being wheeled to an ambulance. Her mind immediately went to Peter and the children. Thoughts racing, she looked from left to right and tried to sit up. The gurney straps held her tight. She trembled with panic.

She asked one of the paramedics, "Where are my kids? Is my husband alive?"

The man she spoke to leaned in. He said, "Everything is going to be okay, Miss. Try to relax. We're going to the hospital."

"I'm not hurt. I want to see my kids. I want to know if my husband is alright."

They reached the ambulance and the men hoisted the gurney into the vehicle and sat beside her. She asked, "Please, could you tell me if my husband is alive?"

There was a look of sadness in the man's eyes. He said, "Your husband didn't make it, Mrs. Apple. The children are with social services. They had your neighbors call for help and we found you passed out. Can I ask why you shot the man in your room?"

"He was chasing me. He shot my husband. Is he dead?"

"He's dead, ma'am, I'm going to need you to relax. We're going to take care of you."

Chloe shivered and tears began to flow. Her Peter was gone. Life would never be the same and she wasn't sure how she would be able to go on. She began wishing that she had died too. Grief overtook her. Closing her eyes, she felt the vehicle begin to move. Focusing on the movement, she tried not to think about anything. The emptiness she felt inside was like a black hole sucking her soul into oblivion.

83

At the hospital, after being cleaned up, Chloe was put into a private room. Two men walked in whom she didn't recognize. They were wearing suits and badges. The men introduced themselves as detectives Bard and Simpson. Detective Simpson asked, "Do you have any idea why someone would want to shoot your husband?"

Chloe answered, "He got into a fight with a man at work. Is that who he was?"

"We're not sure, ma'am. That's what we're trying to figure out."

"Can't you ID the man in my home? The man I shot?"

"Mrs. Apple. I'm sorry to have to tell you, but you shot an off duty paramedic. Our guess is that he was trying to help you. What I can tell you is he's not the shooter."

Chloe felt devastated. Not only had she lost her husband, she shot an innocent man. Grief made her stomach turn and tears begin to flow. She wished she could tell the detectives to leave. Knowing they had questions that could lead them to catching Peter's killer was all that kept her from screaming for privacy.

Detective Bard asked, "Can you tell us anything about the man your husband had an altercation with?"

Chloe told the whole story, beginning with Barry and the school, ending with what Peter told her the night before. They took notes and left. She curled herself into a ball and pulled the sheets tight around her body. Violent trembles took over her entire being. She prayed for Peter and the man she'd shot. The thought that she had become a murderer on the day her husband died plagued her conscience. Crying with intensity, exhaustion took over. Falling asleep she could see Peter, in her mind's eye, smiling the moment before he'd been shot.

84

Mila gave the social worker the only number she had memorized and could think of, Rebecca's. She sat quietly and sorrowfully with Barry in the bland room of the children's hospital. The thoughts running through her mind were random. She didn't understand why the staff was so evasive when she asked about her mother and father. All they had were cookie cutter responses. Barry wouldn't say a word. She watched him stare at the wall, distant and cold. Trying to make sense of it all seemed useless and the situation felt hopeless to her.

When Rebecca entered the room, Mila streaked across and wrapped herself around Rebecca's waist. Something inside her wanted to believe that the woman could make it better. She thought that Rebecca could give her answers, sort everything out, and protect her from the monster that had become her imagination.

Rebecca knelt down and looked Mila in the eyes. She said, "I want you to be strong, baby. I have some news and it's not good."

Mila wiped her eyes. "I don't want it to be bad news."

"Baby, I have to tell you something that's going to hurt. Let's go sit over there on the bed with your brother and we can talk about it together."

Mila and Rebecca sat next to Barry, Rebecca in the middle. Rebecca said, "I know you two are going through a lot right now. I don't like to be the one telling you this, but the doctors wanted you to hear it from someone you know."

Mila asked, "What is it, Aunt Rebecca? I'm so scared."

"I know, baby. It's really bad. Your father isn't with us anymore."

"What do you mean?" Mila cried with fury. "I don't understand."

"He's dead, Mila. He's gone."

Barry stood without a word and went to the bedside table. Pulling the drawer out, he threw it on the floor.

85

When the doctor entered Chloe's room, she sat up in bed. He said, "I'm Doctor Brad Brooke. I can see on your charts that you sustained no physical injuries."

Chloe asked, "Can I go? I want to be with my children."

"I think it's best that you get a psychiatric evaluation. Is there anyone you'd like to contact?"

Chloe thought for a moment. "Peter's parents. They need to know what's going on."

"Very well, Mrs. Apple. There's a phone right there, bedside. Have you used it?"

"No. I didn't even think about calling anyone. I feel so confused. It's like this is all a nightmare. I can still see my husband's face, and I don't want to believe he's gone."

"That's understandable, Mrs. Apple. You need support now. Anyone who would care about you and your situation should be contacted. Unfortunately, you and your husband both only have each other listed as emergency contacts. We aren't going to dig anyone up. What's your relationship like with your in-laws?"

"Not so good. I think it's been two or three years since we've talked. Peter's dad is very strict. They use to butt heads a lot."

Tears began streaking down Chloe's cheeks. She didn't like the thought that Peter would never have another opportunity to make amends with his father. Thinking about how much his mother disliked her made her cringe, too. Having to be the one to call them wasn't what she wanted. She knew that she and the kids would probably end up living with them, though. The thought of going back and trying to live in the house Peter had been murdered in didn't appeal to her.

Dr. Brooke said, "I'm going to leave and give you some time to make phone calls. If you need directory assistance, dial zero or just dial nine to call out. I'll be back in about an hour and we'll talk about admitting you to psychiatric services for a few days."

"I don't want to go to psychiatric services."

"Mrs. Apple. It would be unfortunate for you to leave the hospital's care without a proper evaluation. There are going to be some issues after witnessing what you did. It would be a miracle if there weren't. Things like sleeping problems and depression. We just want to observe you for forty-eight to seventy-two hours. I know there are things that will need to be done concerning your husband. That's why I'm urging you to call for support and cooperate with us concerning your mental health."

"Okay. I'll do it. What about my children?"

"I need a signature from a guardian concerning their

care."

The doctor passed her a clip board. He said, "We have this form saying a Mrs. Rebecca Frost can make decisions concerning them. Unless you would rather leave the responsibility with your in-laws when they arrive."

"How did you get Rebecca's info? I thought you weren't going to dig anyone up."

"She's who your children asked for. Your daughter gave us her number, and she's with them now. If you don't trust her to make decisions for them, we can wait."

Chloe bit her lip. She said, "I trust her. I don't want to give up my children, though."

"It's nothing like that, Mrs. Apple. It's only concerning treatment."

"Okay."

Chloe signed the papers and handed them back to the doctor. He said, "I'll go now. Make as many calls as you need to."

The doctor left and Chloe picked up the phone's receiver. Dialing Peter's parents, her hands shook so violently she could hardly complete the action. There were a couple of rings and his mother answered. Chloe tried to speak but all she could do is sob. When the wrenching cries subsided, she told Peter's mother, Samantha, what happened.

86

Rebecca lay in the hospital bed holding Barry. Mila rested snugly against her side, sniffling. They lay quietly. Rebecca wished she knew what to say, but she couldn't find the words. The nurse came in. In a soft spoken tone, the nurse said, "Visitation is over, Mrs. Frost."

Mila began crying again. Rebecca said, "Don't worry, baby. I'll be here first thing in the morning."

Barry said, "I don't want you to go. Why won't they let you stay with us?"

The nurse said, "It's policy, dear. I'm sure she'll be back."

Rebecca stood and readied herself to leave. The nurse left the room and gave her an opportunity to talk to the children alone. Mila gripped her waist. It hurt Rebecca to leave them.

Mila said, "I love you, Aunt Rebecca. Please come back."

Tears threatened to spill from Rebecca's eyes. The children seemed so helpless and she didn't know exactly how to deal with it. She wasn't an overly emotional person, so the feelings she was experiencing made her uncomfortable. Most of her life she had run from or avoided anything that made her feel raw emotion. She wasn't going to abandon the children, though. Doing her best not to show her sadness, she knelt down to speak with Mila.

Rebecca said, "Baby, you have to be strong. Take care of your brother and I'll be back as soon as I'm allowed to, I promise."

Mila wiped her eyes. She said, "I want to go home with you. I don't want to stay here. I want my mommy."

"I'll check on your mommy tomorrow, before I come here. Would you like that?"

"I just want to know if she's okay. I'm so scared."

"Don't be scared, baby. The hospital is going to take care of you. You let me know if anyone mistreats you, okay? I'll sock 'em."

Mila smiled. She said, "You're funny."

"I'm not being funny, baby. I'll kick their butts."

Barry said, "You're not supposed to hit people."

Rebecca smirked. She said, "A lesson some of us have a hard time learning. I want to hear it from both of you. I want you to say you'll be strong."

The children looked at each other. Rebecca said, "Say it."

Both the children spoke at once. "We'll be strong."

"Beautiful. I'm going to make sure you're treated right, and I'll be here for you all the way. Okay?"

Mila hugged Rebecca's neck. She said, "I'm going to miss you, Aunt Rebecca. Please come back."

Rebecca's heart crumbled. She said, "I'll be back,

baby. I promise

87

Detectives Bard and Simpson sat outside the Craig residence. Around 2:30 am a green pickup with camper shell swerved into the driveway. They exited their police car to confront the suspect. Guns drawn, they approached the vehicle with caution. The man behind the wheel seemed to be having trouble getting out of the vehicle. It was apparent he was inebriated.

Detective Bard spoke loudly. He said, "Elvin Craig! This is detective Bard with the Dallas police department. Show me your hands."

Elvin showed no signs of comprehension. He opened the truck door and fell to the ground, motionless. Detective Bard approached cautiously, knelt down and checked his pulse, then looked in the cab of the truck. A high powered rifle with scope sat in plain view. The detective put Elvin Craig in cuffs, then called for a crime scene investigation unit to collect evidence. He had no doubts that they had found their shooter.

88

Waking in the holding cell, Elvin Craig Sr. became angry and vocal. He yelled, "What the fuck! Hello, officers! What the fuck am I doing here?"

A detention officer came to his cell door. He said, "Oh, look. The asshole's awake. Ready to get booked in, prick?"

"Hey, what the fuck's wrong with you, motherfucker? Let me outta here you son of a bitch."

The detention officer laughed. He said, "You ain't goin' nowhere. You're gonna rot in one of these cells, you murdering bastard. The detectives are gonna talk to you soon. It's all over the news, you gunned down a man long range in front of his wife and kids. I hope you get the fuckin' death penalty. Now, shut the fuck up and we'll start book in, soon."

"I didn't murder no-one."

"We'll see about that."

Elvin sat in the plain white room and stared at the mirror. Detectives Bard and Simpson stood behind the two-way glass and looked into his eyes. Detective Bard said, "This guy has no remorse. We've got all the evidence we need, but I want a confession. What do you think?"

Simpson grunted. He was the 260-pound gym rat that couldn't stand a bully or a murderer. He said, "You know what I think. I think it'd be nice to turn the cameras off and knock all the teeth out this bastard's head."

When the detectives walked into the room, Elvin Craig said, "This is a setup and you know it. I haven't done shit."

Detective Simpson said, "We don't want to hear any of your innocence bullshit. We want to know what possessed you to do what you did. We've got all the evidence we need to cook your ass. Tell us why you shot a man in front of his family."

"I'm not tellin' you shit. Put me in my cell. I'm only talkin' to my lawyer."

Detective Bard said, "We'll put you in your cell, and we'll see you in court."

89

Chloe couldn't sleep. She sat in the mental observation ward and stared out the window. It was raining lightly, and there was something comforting about that to her. It was as though the sky cried for her and all she had to do was watch misery fall and drench the world that seemed so grotesque and distant now. Other patients wandered about or sat around in reclining chairs. A cold lump lodged in her throat. The pain she felt could not have a name to her, it was indescribable. She thought about all the years Peter had been her rock. His absence left her incomplete.

A nurse approached carrying a small plastic cup with pills in it and a paper cup with water. She said, "The doctor prescribed these for you. You haven't slept and he ordered a sedative and something to help you with racing thoughts. Want to give them a try?"

Chloe took the cups from the nurse and swallowed the pills. She handed the empty containers back to the nurse and the nurse left her to her thoughts. Chloe thought, if she had the opportunity to jump from the top of the building, she would. The only thing that countered the suicidal thoughts was her belief that suicide was against God. Her anguish, although formidable, wouldn't end that way; nevertheless, the thought kept returning.

Come sunrise, the nurse returned to where Chloe sat. She said, "You have visitors."

"Who is it?"

"Martin and Samantha Apple. I believe they're your in-laws. Correct?"

"Yes."

"Would you like to see them?"

"Yes. That's fine."

"Okay. You'll need to come to the day room to visit."

Chloe went to the dayroom and Martin and Samantha were brought in. Chloe's breath left her for a moment. She'd never realized how much Peter resembled his father until now. Everything about the man reminded her of him. It brought tears to her eyes and before the couple sat, the tears flowed. Samantha joined in a cry of grief. She hugged Chloe tight.

Peter's father showed no emotion. He said, "They arrested the man that shot Peter. Found the gun in his truck. The guy was so drunk he passed out on the lawn and they had to carry him to the squad car. It was all over the news. They're gonna fry that guy."

Chloe didn't say a word. She felt relieved to hear that the police had arrested the man responsible. It made her think of the innocent man she'd shot. The vision of him clutching his wounds, blood pouring out of him, haunted her. How could she forgive herself? Everything was like a waking nightmare she just couldn't escape.

Samantha asked, "How are you holding up, Chloe? Is there anything we can do?"

"Can you bring Peter back to life? Can you bring the man I shot back to life?"

Samantha covered her mouth. Martin said, "You know that's not possible. We're here to help, but you have to be realistic. She's asking if you need anything."

Chloe said, "Right now, I just want to be able to stop thinking. I don't think anyone can help with that."

The rest of the visit went with long lapses of silence. When the couple left, Chloe felt relieved that she didn't have to communicate anymore. She wanted to stare out the window at the gloomy day which was her only reprieve.

When she got another visit it came as a shock to her system. Having Rebecca see her in the condition she was in didn't appeal to Chloe. Allowing the visit, Chloe went to the dayroom. Rebecca came in and sat next to her. Rebecca asked, "How are you doing, baby?"

"I'm not doing so well."

"Well. I'm going to see the kids after this. Is there anything you want to tell them?"

"I don't know what to say."

"Say everything's going to be okay."

"Is it?"

"Eventually it will be. The horror of seeing Peter murdered will probably never leave you, but you all have to go on. That might sound harsh or trite, but it's true. You know that, right?"

"I guess. I just don't know how I'm going to move forward. It's all a shock to the system, I don't see how I can recover from it."

"I'll help you."

"How?"

"Any way I can. You have to promise me something though."

"I don't know if I can uphold any promises right now."

"Just promise you'll do your best to be strong. That's what I need to hear. For the kids."

"I'll be strong. I'm not sure how. For the kids I'll do my best, though."

"Beautiful. That's what I needed to hear."

Rebecca hugged Chloe. She kissed her on the cheek, then held her at arm's length. She said, "All you need. Anything you need. You ask me. Okay?"

"I don't think you can give me all I need."

"I can give you more than you think, baby. I'm here for you."

"I believe you."

"Good. I've got to get to the kids. I'll visit again later. Okay?"

"Okay."

Chloe watched Rebecca leave and found herself thinking how lucky she was to have met her. In her current state of mind, it felt good to focus on something other than the revolving thoughts of Peter and the dead paramedic. Knowing she wouldn't have to go through it all alone afforded a small amount of comfort that she needed to stay sane. She began feeling the effects of the medication, and with the thought that maybe everything would somehow get better with Rebecca's help, Chloe fell into a deep sleep

90

Mila sat in the quiet room holding Barry's hand. He wouldn't talk. Only moments ago he allowed her to hold his hand. He stared at the wall, and Mila wondered if he envisioned the same thing that her mind could not escape. She had lain in the hospital bed with her eyes closed but her mind never stopped churning. The vision of her father's chest exploding haunted her. His smile. His white teeth. The blood. She wondered if Barry had slept because she wasn't sure she had. Not knowing what he was thinking, Mila periodically tried to get him to say something, her efforts procuring nothing but silence.

Rebecca walked in and Mila's heart fluttered. She let go of Barry's hand and ran to her. Rebecca hugged her and Mila felt secure for the first time in an hour, since her grandparents' visit. Tears flowed down her small cheeks.

Mila said, "I told my granny and pawpaw about you. I'm so glad you're back."

"Why wouldn't I be, baby? I told you I wouldn't abandon you."

"Granny said not to depend on anyone. She said we were going with her. I want to go with you."

"I don't know if you can come with me, baby. You might have to go with your grandma."

"What about my mommy?"

"Your mommy is being strong, just like you. I don't know what she's going to do yet. I promise everything will be okay in time, though, baby. You have to trust me."

"I don't like it at grandma's, though."

"Baby, it's probably where you're going to have to be for a while."

"What about my mommy?"

"She'll probably be there, too. Right now she has to get better."

"You said she was being strong. Why can't she have us?"

"She will, baby. Just give things time. This is a horrible situation."

"I know." Mila cried. Her face screwed and she grew angry. She screamed, "Why is this happening? I've been good. I've always been good. Why did my daddy have to die?"

Rebecca knelt down and looked Mila in the eye. She said, "None of this is your fault, baby. A terrible man caused this."

"I don't understand. Why did God let this happen?"

"I don't know why God lets things like this happen, baby. Tell me you'll be strong."

"I don't want to be strong. I want my daddy."

Rebecca embraced Mila. The thoughts churning in Mila's mind were relentless. She felt submerged in confusion and disbelief. Barry stood and began punching the wall, screaming. Nurses rushed in from the hallway and subdued him. Mila wiped her eyes and watched the staff strap Barry into a strait jacket board. There were no words to express her grief. She watched silently as the staff left with him.

Rebecca said, "You see why you have to be strong. Your brother needs you."

"I'll be strong."

Rebecca hugged Mila. "Beautiful."

91

Three days passed and the children were released to their grandparents' custody. Chloe sat alone on the hospital bed, morose but ready to leave the place. She didn't want to go to her in-laws' home. Rebecca picked her up and guilt ate at Chloe. She felt like she was abandoning the children. All the paperwork had been signed to give Martin and Samantha temporary custody of them. The suggestion came from Martin and Samantha. Chloe felt it was the right thing to do for the moment. She signed them over for six months. Leaving the hospital, the world looked odd to Chloe. Everything seemed dimmer, almost meaningless.

Rebecca asked, "How are you feeling, baby?"

"I feel like crap."

"Did they give you some good meds?"

"I guess. Anxiety pills. Sleeping pills. Depression pills. Pills, pills, pills. I don't see how they're going to make my life better. How am I supposed to function on all of this?"

"They gave them to you for a reason, baby. Give them a try for a while. Eventually you might not need any."

"I do need to sleep. We have to fill the prescriptions."

"Beautiful. We'll pass by the pharmacy on the way home."

"Home? I don't have a home."

"Home is wherever you make it, baby."

"I'll never have another home without Peter." Chloe's eyes filled with tears.

Rebecca said, "Baby, I'm here. I don't know how much that means to you, but I'm going to be here as long as you need me."

"Great. Get ready for a long stay. I'm completely destroyed."

"However long it takes, baby. Period."

"The funeral is tomorrow. Is it horrible that I don't want to go?"

"It's natural, baby. Who's happy about seeing the love of their life buried? You have to go. Barry and Mila will be there; imagine how they feel."

"You're right. I have to."

"Beautiful. Now, let's get some medication."

92

The smoldering summer sun induced sweat from all who attended Peter's funeral. Leave it to Texas weather to be raining and gloomy one day and bright and shiny the next, with humidity that could suffocate a person to death. People fanned themselves in their black attire. There were people there whom Chloe wasn't familiar with. Most of them were Peter's parents' friends. Some of them she remembered from her and Peter's wedding. There were people from Peter's work, some of whom she'd met at Christmas parties and other company functions. Most she vaguely recognized. Almost everyone gave condolences at the reception.

She didn't like how there were those who seemed to be ogling her at moments. She could see pity in their eyes and it made her wish she was invisible. The flowers didn't smell pretty to her, they smelled like death. Everything and everyone surrounding her smelled like death. Murder clouded her mind. Thinking of herself as a murderer, attending the funeral of her murdered husband, made her nauseous. Bile lodged in her throat.

When the service was over, she said her goodbyes to

the children. Mila asked, "When are you gonna come get us?"

Chloe was shaking. The sight of Peter being lowered into the ground had put her on the verge of a nervous breakdown. She wanted to be in the casket with him. She told Mila, "I don't know, sweetie. Aren't your grandma and grandpa taking care of you?"

"I want you, Mommy. I don't want to live there."

"It's temporary, sweetie. I promise."

"So you're getting better?"

Tears welled in Chloe's eyes. She said, "I'm going to get better, honey." She bit her lip. She said, "Be patient, sweetie, please."

"I was there, too. Why are you running away?"

"Mila. I'm not discussing this now."

"When? When can we talk about it? Barry doesn't say nothing. He breaks everything, you know. He knows that boy's daddy did this. He thinks it's all his fault."

Chloe wiped her eyes. She said, "Maybe it is his fault." She turned and walked away.

Mila screamed, "Mommy, don't leave me!" Her grandmother grabbed her.

Chloe climbed into Rebecca's car and they drove away.

93

At Rebecca's apartment, classical music filled the air. Chloe hadn't been out of bed in three days. Trying to respect her wishes, Rebecca had given her as much space as possible. Now she'd had enough. Knocking on the bedroom door, she'd gotten no answer for the fifth time in the day. The sudden thought Chloe was dead behind the locked door startled Rebecca into action.

She went to the kitchen and retrieved a butter knife to jimmy the lock. Going back to the room, she knocked once again with resounding thumps. She said, "Chloe, I'm coming in." There was no answer, so she wedged the knife in the door, opening it.

Her eyes had to adjust to the dark. She could see Chloe lying on the bed. Walking over to where her friend lay, Rebecca reached out to touch her. Chloe sat up, a wild look on her face and in her eyes showing from the hallway light aglow on her features.

Chloe said, "I told you not to disturb me."

Rebecca said, "Baby, I'm here to help. You haven't eaten or showered in days. This room is funky, and when I said I'd help, I didn't mean help you wither away and die."

"Well, what the hell am I supposed to do? I'm depressed and devastated. All I want to do is sleep and when I sleep all I have is nightmares."

"I tell you what, baby. You get in the shower, I'll clean and deodorize this room, and then we'll have drinks."

"I don't want to go anywhere."

"We'll have sandwiches and drinks in the living room. Please, baby, this is a bad program. You're not going to start feeling better laying around withering away in sorrows. Trust me. Get in the shower and we'll go from there. I'll take care of everything."

Chloe crawled out of bed. She said, "My whole body aches."

"I can imagine. I put all your clothes away for you the other day, before you locked the door. Do you remember? I bought you some really nice things."

"I could be in silk or rags; I wouldn't feel any better."

"Let's give silk a try, baby."

"I guess."

"Beautiful."

94

Mila sat staring at the cat outside of her grandmother's living room window. It was a stray. Her grandmother fed the stray cats sometimes, so they kept coming back. There were five of them. The only one there at the moment was a scrawny grey and black female. There were patches of fur missing from the vagrant's coat and it had fresh scratch marks on its face from some kind of brawl, apparently.

Watching the cat made Mila think of herself. She could see similarities between herself and the animal. The one that came to mind first was that, in a way, they were both strays—damaged strays—living off the helping hand of her grandmother. Her grandmother didn't do much else than feed the cats, just as she would feed her and Barry. Depression set in and Mila went to the small room she shared with her brother.

Entering the room, she saw Barry busy in the corner. Walking up to see what had him occupied, she could see he had one of her dolls. What he was doing to the toy disturbed her extremely. He had a knife carving the face away. One of the eyes had been removed and the nose, gone. Working on shaving an ear off, he didn't even turn to see who stood behind him.

Mila asked, "Boo-boo, are you okay?"

Barry stuck the knife in the wall with complete disregard to the damage it caused the sheet rock. He turned with a maniacal grin on his face. He said, "We should run away. They wouldn't even care if we were gone. We could live in the woods and kill animals to eat."

Mila sat next to him and took his hand in hers. She said, "Mommy's coming back for us. You'll see."

"Poppa isn't coming back. You saw, they put him in the ground. I want to dig him up."

"That wouldn't help, boo-boo. He's gone."

"I don't wanna start school here, sissy. I don't ever want to go to school again."

"We have to. Maybe mommy will homeschool us when she gets better."

"What about us? We're not better. We're worser than ever. Let's run away."

"No, boo-boo. We have to stay here and wait for mommy and Aunt Rebecca."

Barry frowned deeply. He shook his head. "They ain't comin' back. We're on our own."

Tears rolled down Mila's face. She said, "Don't say things like that. It's mean. I believe they're coming back."

95

Chloe allowed the hot water to wash over her shoulders and roll down her back. Steam rose and cleared her sinuses from congestion due to days of sleeping and weeping. Shaking inside and wondering what it'd be like to drown, she shut the water off and took a towel off the rack to dry herself. On the counter she found a silk nightgown folded neatly, waiting for her. She hadn't even heard Rebecca enter.

She found her friend sitting in one of the plush chairs in the living room waiting for her. Rebecca said, "There she is. Come sit, baby. I toasted your bread. Tuna and cheese. Is that okay?"

Chloe sat with a slump. "Yeah, that's fine."

"Beautiful. Tell me something."

"Please don't ask me to say I'll be strong."

"I'm not. Tell me something you want. Something you've always wanted."

"I don't know."

"You know, baby. Think about it. Anything. Something you wanted to do with Peter, or before him. Something you fantasize about. Anything."

Chloe thought for a moment. She bit her lip. "I always wanted to travel."

"Where?"

"Beaches. I love beaches. I've only been to Galveston and Padre."

"Beautiful. That's a start. I'll get the laptop and we can look at some places."

"We can't go."

"Yes we can."

"I don't know if I can. I feel horrible."

Rebecca shook her head. She said, "Baby, if we had to feel perfect to do things we'd never get anything done."

Chloe huffed. "These are extreme circumstances. It's not like my dog died, Becca. My husband died."

"I know, baby. Sitting in a room dying inside isn't going to make you feel better, though."

Chloe looked at her hands and began fidgeting. Rebecca said, "I see the wheels spinning. What are you thinking?"

"I'd like to go to Cancun. I always wanted to."

"Beautiful. We'll plan it all out. You and me. We have to get your mind off the wretched things you've experienced."

"What about my psychiatrist? I have appointments."

"Your next appointment is in two days. We'll go to that, then Mexico, baby."

Chloe smiled. She said, "You're such a rebel, Becca."

"Oh, baby. You have no idea, but you will."

96

Elvin Craig sat in his cell. He was in general population now, the other inmates asking him a million questions. Walking out into the day room, he joined a card game. One of the men said, "You're a mutherfuckin' cheat. I'm not playin' cards with some asshole who'd shoot a man in the back, long distance, in front of his children. Get the fuck away from my table, asshole."

Elvin rose from the game table and wandered across the room. A few moments later, he streaked back across the room and swooped up a chair. The cheap plastic broke on the back of the man's skull, pieces flying like shrapnel. The group of men playing all attacked at once. Guards flooded the tank and were liberal with the pepper spray.

Underneath the dog pile, they picked Elvin up. Beaten, bruised and bloody—he grinned on his way to solitary confinement.

97

Mila sat across from her grandmother at the kitchen table. Samantha said, "In a couple of weeks, you're going to go back to school. How do you feel about that?"

Mila stared at the mutilated doll in the middle of the table. It looked like a nightmare. She had become well acquainted with nightmares lately. Tears flowed and streamed down her pale cheeks. Wiping her nose, she looked up. Shaking her head, thinking about all the violence that had destroyed her life, she couldn't find the words to say how distressed she felt.

Samantha asked, "What happened to this doll?"

"I don't want to talk about it."

"Did you do this?"

"It doesn't matter. You don't understand."

Samantha picked the toy up and examined it. She said, "This type of behavior is unacceptable. We have to talk about it."

Mila put her face in her hands. She screamed, "I hate it here!"

Samantha remained calm. She said, "Where else are

you going to be, Mila? Do you want to go into foster care?"

"I don't know. I want to be with my mommy. I told you that."

Samantha clucked, false teeth clacking. She said, "You're with us for a few months. You might be with us permanently. It's something you and Barry are going to have to get used to."

"How can we? You want us to act like nothing happened and it did. A lot happened and I'm not okay. Why are we being punished? Our daddy died in front of us and you want us to be normal. I don't understand."

"Listen, Mila. We want what's best for you. Eventually you have to move on and we're not going to baby you. You still have to go to school and do everything every other child has to do. Chores, homework, go to bed on time. These are all things you must do."

"You're mean. My mommy doesn't want to come here with us because you and grandpa are both mean. It's why we didn't see you for so long. They don't like you, and I don't either."

Samantha put her hand to her chest. She said, "How dare you, young lady. You don't get to talk to me like that. I ought to make you go into the garden and pick a switch. I know you're hurting right now, so I think you need to go to your room and think long and hard about what you just said to me."

Mila left the table and went to her room. She sat on the edge of the bed next to Barry. She said, "Maybe we will run away, boo-boo."

98

Fidgeting, Chloe bit her lip and sighed as she sat in the psychiatrist's office. She didn't want to talk about what happened, again. Thinking about Peter and the man she shot made her sick inside. Being in the presence of the doctor was like going to court for the murder of both her husband and the paramedic. Thinking about it seemed to be all she did lately. The thoughts brought tears to her eyes.

The doctor asked, "Have you talked to your children lately?"

Chloe spoke out of the side of her mouth, "Yeah, I talk to them." The lie made her feel lousy. It would make her feel even worse to admit and have to talk about why she didn't want to see them.

The doctor asked, "How are they?"

Chloe looked at her hands and twiddled her thumbs. She said, "They're okay, I guess. I mean, what do you expect? They watched their father die."

"You watched your husband die. Tell me how that makes you feel."

"Well, Dr. Blanch. I'll tell you. I feel pitiful. I want

to be dead. The memory of that moment when the blood hit my face is haunting me. I still feel the blood on my face sometimes. I wake up sweating and I think I'm covered in it. I wipe and wipe but it never seems to come off me. I'm always covered in it."

"What about the man you shot? The paramedic." Dr. Blanch looked at his notes. He said, "Benjamin Watts. He was your neighbor. An innocent man. How does it make you feel?"

Chloe stood. She said, "I don't want to talk anymore. Can you give me my prescription?"

"Please, Mrs. Apple. Sit."

"I don't think so. Forget about it. I'm leaving."

"Okay. Let me write a script. Will you sit while I do that?"

Chloe sat and began fidgeting again. The doctor wrote a script and passed it to her. He said, "Make an appointment with my secretary before you leave."

"I'm not sure I want to do that."

"You need someone to talk to. These thoughts and feelings you have aren't going to go away on their own. I'm here to help."

"I'll make an appointment, but I'm leaving town."

"Oh. How long will you be gone?"

"I don't know yet."

"Okay. Let me see that script."

"You're not going to help me now?"

"I'm going to make your script for ninety days."

Dr. Blanch wrote the new script and handed it to her. He said, "I want you to make the appointment for thirty days. If you're not in my office then, I'll expect to see you in ninety days, even if it's just for another script. I do recommend a full session."

Chloe left the office and made her appointment. She thought Dr. Blanch was okay. Talking about Peter and the paramedic hurt, but she told herself she would try harder to participate in counseling when she returned. Walking up to Rebecca's car she could hear loud rap music. She smiled to herself. Her friend was odd, and she loved it.

Sitting in the passenger seat, Rebecca turned down her music. She asked, "How did it go?"

Chloe said, "It went like crap, I guess."

"Why, baby?"

"I just don't want to talk about that day. It's all I think about."

"I'm sorry. What do you want to do now?"

"I want to go to the beach."

"Car or plane?"

"Let's drive."

Rebecca started the car. She said, "We'll need cash. I've got something to show you."

99

Barry had his backpack loaded with things he wanted to run away with. He asked Mila, "Can we leave tonight?"

Mila said, "I don't know, boo-boo. Where are we gonna go?"

"Anywhere. We can build a tree house in the park."

"They'll find us there. It's only a couple of blocks away."

"Then let's go home. I wanna go home."

Mila shook her head. She said, "I don't want to be in that house."

Barry asked, "Have you talked to momma?"

"She won't talk to me. Aunt Rebecca says she's getting better, though. Maybe we should wait here for her."

Barry dropped his backpack. He said, "You said we could leave. You're a liar."

He went to the corner and sat, crossing his arms, staring at her in a way that made her not want to sleep in the same room with him. She asked, "What are you thinking?"

"You don't wanna know what I'm thinking."

"Well. Stop it. You scare me."

"I oughta scare you. I don't want to be here. If I don't leave, I'm gonna kill grandma."

Mila started crying. She said, "Don't say things like that, boo-boo. It's so ugly."

"What do you want me to say? I hate it here."

"Say you'll stay with me. Say you won't do anything crazy."

"I wanna leave."

"I know, boo-boo. We need to stay, though. You need to be good."

Barry stood and climbed onto the bed next to her. He said, "I love you, sissy." He hugged her. Feeling Mila shaking made him think about what he said. Thinking about how badly he wanted to leave, but how badly he wanted to be with his sister made him feel regret. He said, "I'm sorry. I'll be good."

Mila hugged him back. She said, "Please, boo-boo. Don't scare me."

"I'm sorry."

100

Rebecca pulled into the apartment complex and parked. She said, "What I'm going to show you and tell you might come as a shock."

"Tell me."

Rebecca opened her car door and stepped out. She peeked her head back into the car. She said, "Come on, baby. Time for an adventure. I'll tell you everything when we get there."

"What do you mean? Are we taking a cab?"

"No. I have a truck. We take it to get there. I don't like driving the Lexus on dirt roads."

Chloe's interest was piqued. What did this curious woman have in store? How much was she hiding? A truck? Dirt roads. Where could she be taking her?

Chloe exited the vehicle and followed Rebecca to an apartment garage. Rebecca pulled a remote from her purse and pressed a button. The metal door whined and began to lift. What was behind it looked like a monster of a truck. Pink and black paintjob and large black wheels. It looked like it shouldn't even be able to fit in the garage. The big pink Chevy bowtie in the grill was almost at eye level.

Chloe asked, "Do we really need something like this to get where we're going?"

Rebecca laughed. She looked at Chloe with the ever-so-familiar curious look she had when it seemed like she could size a person up through those eagle eyes at a glance. Sometimes Chloe wondered just what kind of a predator her dear friend was—certain that the Asian beauty was a predator. The thought of what Rebecca might be capable of excited her.

Chloe said, "We should get a few things. Shouldn't we?"

"Trust me, baby. We have all we need, and we can buy everything else. Rebecca touched another button on the keys and the monster truck issued a chirp. Chloe jumped, startled. Rebecca said, "Let's go, baby. Adventure awaits."

Chloe went to the passenger door and climbed into the heavy-duty machine. Rebecca settled in the driver's seat and turned the ignition. Roaring to life, the lope of the big motor and the growl of its exhaust made the interior rumble. Putting the truck in gear, Rebecca pulled out of the garage and pressed a button to close the door.

Rebecca asked, "Are you ready?"

"I don't think I could be more ready than I am now."

Rebecca pushed the gas and the truck grumbled out of the parking lot and on to the main road. Turning up the radio, Rebecca grinned at Chloe. Heavy metal screamed from the speakers, treble and bass rumbling through the cab. Chloe recognized the band—Pantera. She smiled and Rebecca turned it up further. Entering the highway, she smashed the gas. Chloe liked the feeling of adrenaline flowing through her as the force of the vehicle's acceleration pushed her into the seat.

101

Elvin Craig Sr. sat in his single cell in the North Tower, Lew Sterrett Justice Center. He ate the mystery meat from his tray and listened to the inmates in the dayroom argue about what channel to watch. The cell he occupied in the psych ward was small but an improvement over his previous one. There were no card games, but he didn't care. His door could be locked whenever he wanted. A little green button beside the door would let him out any time he wanted before 10pm.

Finishing his meager meal, he brought his tray out to the front and left it to be picked up, avoiding eye contact with the other men. Elvin didn't like anyone. He wasn't the sociable type. Thinking how much he hated the place, but that he would be spending a lot of time there, he occupied himself with drawing. He knew he might be getting a life sentence. The thought of the death penalty felt more comforting.

102

Barry and Mila sat at the kitchen table with their grandparents, the mood heavy like a cloak of frustration and chaos. Martin and Samantha Apple were livid. A look of disgust veiled Grandpa Martin's face. He said, "If neither of you own up to this you'll both be punished."

The children sat quiet. Samantha asked, "Who defecated on the living room carpet?"

Mila said, "Maybe someone broke in, or one of your cats."

Martin said, "That isn't cat poop and you know it. One of you is cleaning up that mess."

Mila said, "I'll clean it."

Samantha said, "No. Your brother will. We know he did it. Since both of you want to play dumb, no more toys or cartoons for the week."

Martin said, "Mila, you go to the room and start collecting all the toys. Barry, get some toilet paper and clean the mess on the floor."

The children stood and went to do what they were told. When Barry finished with the mess he joined Mila in the room to help clean out anything that could be considered a toy. Mila's frustration poured over. She said, "You told me you were going to be good."

Barry said, "She made me eat everything on my plate again last night. I was mad."

"You can't do things like this. I have to suffer, too. Don't you understand? They're hard enough to live with."

"I know. I think we should go."

"Boo-boo, we're not goin' anywhere. Get used to it. We're gonna have to try to get along with them."

Barry sat on the bed and Mila sat beside him. They stared at the bag full of toys. Mila said, "Maybe if we're good it won't be so bad here."

"They don't like me."

"I don't think they like me, either, boo-boo. Acting out ain't gonna make them like us any better."

"I'm just not good."

"Don't say that. You can be good. Aunt Rebecca says she's gonna make sure mommy gets us back. Now they're not even gonna let me call, because you had to go poop on the floor. It's not fair."

"Why do you keep calling her? Momma won't even talk to you."

"Aunt Rebecca says she's gettin' better, though. She'll talk to me, soon."

"I'm so mad. It's all my fault."

Mila hugged Barry. "It's not your fault, boo-boo. You thought you had to hit that boy. You didn't know what would happen."

Barry buried his face into Mila and began crying a sorrowful, wretched cry. Mila's heart broke, it was the first time she remembered him crying, since he was a baby.

103

Chloe woke to the truck teetering. She looked out her window and could see thick woods. Yawning and leaning forward she peered out the windshield. They were on a rough dirt road. The big beast of a vehicle took the dips and rises like they were nothing.

Chloe said, "Now I see why the truck."

Rebecca laughed, a wicked and seductive sound. She said, "Baby, a girl has to be prepared."

"Are you going to tell me where we're going, yet? I've got a few thousand in the bank. I could pay for the trip."

"Nonsense. You won't be worried about money in another mile or so."

Chloe processed what Rebecca said. She asked, "If you have so much money, why were you working at a bakery for minimum wage?"

Rebecca looked at Chloe with a curious gleam in her eyes. She said, "I wanted to learn how to bake. Besides, I get bored."

"I get bored, too."

"We all do, baby."

Chloe looked out the passenger side window, watching trees march past like an army of green giants. She wondered what Rebecca planned to show her out in the middle of nowhere. The truck began to slow. Chloe watched as they pulled up to a large cabin.

Rebecca put the truck in park and shut the grumbling motor off. She said, "Ready to see my secret world?"

Chloe asked, "Is this your cabin?"

"Yes."

Chloe felt jittery. She said, "I'm not sure I want to go in. Can you at least give me a clue what I'm walking into?"

"Beautiful. I like how curious you are."

"I don't think I'm all that curious."

"Baby, if you weren't, you wouldn't be here."

Chloe began fidgeting and biting her lip. Rebecca said, "You want to know something before we go inside?"

"Yes."

"I burnt Puff's bakery to the ground."

Chloe's eyes opened wide. She gasped. She asked, "Are you serious?"

"Yes. I robbed them and torched the place."

Shock froze in Chloe's chest. She couldn't think of anything to say. Rebecca said, "I couldn't let them get away with treating you the way they did. Since I couldn't fire them legit, I fired them in a different way. The way those women talked about you when you were gone infuriated me, but I played along."

Chloe shook her head. She said, "You didn't have to do that."

"Oh, baby, they're lucky that's all I did."

Silence filled the cab of the truck. Chloe asked, "What else? What kinds of things do you do?"

"Let's go inside. I want to show you what I've been doing for years."

"You're not a serial killer are you?"

Rebecca laughed her intoxicating laugh and smiled. She said, "Baby, I'm not a serial killer. I am trained, though. I'm going to show you what I'm trained to do."

"Are you going to hurt me?"

A serious look cloaked Rebecca's face and her demeanor changed in such a way that the air seemed to thicken. She said, "I would never hurt you, Chloe. I'm hurt you would think that."

"I don't know what to think."

"I'm going to tell you something you can believe from this day forward. I love you and I would give my life for yours. Don't ever think I would intentionally harm you. I'm going to be there for you as long as you allow me to be. That's the truth. Fact."

Chloe twiddled her thumbs. She looked at her hands and stopped. Breathing deeply, she calmed herself. She said, "Okay. Let's go inside. I want to see."

104

The cabin looked old and somewhat decrepit on its exterior, but inside, the walls were covered in trophies—animal heads, large fish. Rebecca went straight to the thermostat and started the AC. She pulled a cover off a large leather couch and motioned for Chloe to have a seat. The room began to cool as Rebecca wandered off into an adjoining space. She returned momentarily carrying two glasses of wine. Handing one to Chloe, she took a seat next to her on the sofa.

Chloe sipped the red wine and savored the sweet taste. Cool air blew softly against her skin as the place began to feel cozy. Wondering if this was all Rebecca wanted to show her made Chloe smile. Her friend knew how to be mysterious and it piqued her interest. Although the confession about Puff's bakery startled her a bit, she felt loved knowing Rebecca was trying to punish them for mistreating her.

Rebecca said, "When you finish your wine, I'll show you what we came here for."

Chloe gulped. "I thought you wanted to show me

your trophies."

"Aren't they cool? Most of them are my father's."

"Oh, where is he?"

"He passed away a few years ago. He taught me everything I know about hunting and fishing, and the family business."

"That's cool. I never knew my real father."

Rebecca looked at her with those ever so curious eyes. She said, "My father was my world. I'm a total daddy's girl, baby."

"What kind of business was he in?"

Rebecca smirked. She said, "There's that good old curiosity."

"I'm sorry."

"Don't be. Forget about finishing that wine. Come on, I'll show you."

Chloe stood and followed Rebecca to a door underneath the stairway in the hall. Rebecca put her hand on the doorknob. She said, "I'm about to show you something I've never shown anyone. This is my secret world. My father and I built this place and I'm going to give you a tour of our sanctuary. Are you ready?"

"I'm as ready as I'm going to get. Let's go."

Rebecca opened the door and flipped a switch. Florescent lights popped and hummed, lighting a stairway into the bottom of the cabin. Rebecca went inside and Chloe followed her down the stairs. The concrete passage reminded Chloe of an adventure movie. There were expensive looking paintings hanging on the walls. When they reached the bottom of the stairwell, the contents of the room were beyond anything Chloe could have imagined.

The room was filled from wall to wall with weapons. Machine guns on racks. Cases of ammo. Handguns, shotguns, knives and swords. Chloe wondered what someone would need with so many weapons. There were also what looked like artifacts. Stone, jade and gold statues throughout the room.

Rebecca said, "My dad was kind of a survivalist. So am I. Check it out."

Rebecca led Chloe to a door. When she opened it, she revealed a large pantry. The pantry's stock consisted of freeze dried meals and meats, canned goods and liquids from floor to ceiling. Rebecca said, "We could live off this stuff for years if there was some kind of fallout."

Chloe felt exhilarated. She hadn't met anyone in her life as interesting as Rebecca. Wondering what else there could be to see, she bit her lip. Chloe asked, "Is this everything?"

"No. What I brought you here to show you is in the back."

They walked to the back of the basement and Rebecca opened another door and flipped a switch for the lights. An office full of books and a desk occupied the room. Chloe followed Rebecca into the room. She asked, "Have you read all these books?"

"No. Not all of them. My father read most, but some are mine."

Rebecca walked over to the desk and reached under it to press something, then she walked to the book shelf and pulled out a book. When she opened the book it was hollowed out and there was a pad with numbers on it. She pressed some numbers on the pad and the desk began moving to the back wall with an electrical hum. When it rested against the wall, the whine of a motor started and the floor where the desk had sat began to rise.

Chloe stared in amazement at the large safe now protruding from the floor. Rebecca walked up to the safe and spun the dial a few times, she pulled the safe's lever and with a clank it opened, displaying its contents. Awe-struck by what she saw, Chloe's mouth hung open.

Rebecca asked, "What do you think?"

"Is that real gold?"

"Yeah. Mostly twenty-four karat bars. Do you want to hold one?"

"I don't know. I've never seen anything like this. Where did they come from?"

"Well, they're mostly product of the business."

"What business?"

"I'm a burglar, amongst other things."

Rebecca reached down and picked up one of the bars. She handed it to Chloe. She said, "It's okay, baby. The work is done. It's just gold."

Chloe felt the weight of the gold and imagined what it might be worth. She read the markings on it. It read 1 kilo fine gold. She asked, "How much is this worth?"

Rebecca said, "Right now, about forty-thousand."

Chloe had to catch her breath. She said, "You have dozens of them."

"I know. Eighty-two to be exact. About three-mill worth. Rough estimate."

Chloe handed the gold back. She said, "Business must have been good."

"It was."

Rebecca pulled a drawer out of the safe. She said, "Look at these."

Chloe looked in the drawer. It was filled with loose diamonds. Rebecca said, "I'm not even going to get in to how much these are worth." She slid the drawer back in place. Then opened a cabinet. Inside the cabinet were bands of cash.

Rebecca said, "There's a little over five-million in cash here. So, you see, baby—we don't have to worry about money."

105

Mila sat on the bed in a foul mood. She told Barry, "I could call Aunt Rebecca right now if you hadn't done what you did. I'm tired of sitting in this room. How are you gonna feel if they send us away? What if they separate us? What then?"

Barry shook his head. He said, "They won't separate us."

"How do you know? If grandma and grandpa don't keep us, where will we go? You have to be good."

"I will."

"You keep saying that. You still get us both in trouble. I don't like it, boo-boo. I love you, but you're gonna get us put in foster care."

"I won't. I'll be good now. I was just mad."

"You can't do things like poop on the floor when you're mad, or cut things up. I don't know what I'll do if they put us in some place we can't be together. I already worry about you all the time."

"I know, sissy."

Their grandma Samantha entered the room. She said, "I'm not going to let you use the phone or have your toys back yet, but if you want, I'll let y'all watch a program with me and your grandfather."

Mila looked at Barry with question in her expression. Barry said, "We can watch if you want, sissy."

"Yes, I want to."

"Okay."

Samantha smiled. She said, "Great. Let's go to the living room then."

The children walked into the living room and sat on the floor in front of the television. Samantha brought them popcorn and juice to Mila and Barry's surprise. The children smiled at each other and waited for the program to start. When the show came on tears of joy swelled in Mila's eyes. They were watching The Sound of Music, one of her father's favorites. For the first time since his death she felt content. It was as if he were there with her.

106

The road felt comfortable and a peace came over Chloe as they traveled to Mexico. Being at the cabin with Rebecca had opened her eyes to a whole new world. Music filled the cab of the truck and Chloe looked at her friend and smiled. She had no idea why such an exotic and profound creature like Rebecca would find interest in her. She felt fortunate to have her, and she knew that the extraordinary woman would do anything for her.

They pulled into an all-night truck stop with a diner. Rebecca said, "Ready for some cheese burgers? I'm starving."

"Sure. I need to use the restroom and look at myself in the mirror."

"Okay. I'll go with you."

The women walked in and truckers turned and stared. Rebecca said, "I don't think these guys see something as gorgeous as you walk in every day."

Chloe giggled. She said, "I'm pretty sure you're the main attraction. I probably look hideous."

"Nonsense."

Walking to the back of the diner, where the bathrooms were located, Rebecca asked one of the patrons, "Isn't she gorgeous?"

The man nodded his head. He said, "I wouldn't kick her out of my bed."

Rebecca said, "Well, she's mine. Don't make me kick your ass." In a joking tone.

The man said, "No sweat, cookie. I ain't gonna step on yer toes."

Rebecca and the man both laughed. Chloe turned beet red. Rebecca took her arm. She said, "Come on, baby. Let's get freshened up."

107

Mila asked her grandmother, "Can you call my aunt Rebecca and see if my mommy is okay?"

Samantha shook her head. She said, "That woman isn't your aunt. There's no telling what's going on with those two."

"What do you mean? My mommy's gonna get better."

"If she cared she'd be here. I don't care if we don't get along. Your father was my son and she's your mother."

"She'll be here. She's coming back to get us."

"I hope so. Why don't you get cleaned up and make sure your brother washes his hands? I'm going to get lunch ready."

Mila walked away feeling smothered. Getting out of the house is all she could think of. She'd been cooped up all week and it made her feel oppressed. Worse than that, depression had been eating every ounce of strength in her body. Without a release, she thought she might go insane.

In the bedroom, she closed the door behind herself

and slunk down the wall until she sat on the floor. She put her face in her hands and began to cry. Barry came to her side and leaned his head on her. He asked, "What's wrong, sissy?"

Mila looked at him. His blue eyes betrayed little real emotion. He smiled his toothless grin. She ran her fingers through his short blonde hair. She said, "Why is all this happening? Why doesn't mommy want us?"

Barry said, "Because I'm bad."

"It's not all your fault, boo-boo. I'm good. She doesn't want me."

"You said she was gonna get us."

"I just don't know now. Maybe she won't. Maybe we're stuck, boo-boo. What if she never comes back?"

Barry rubbed his face into her shoulder. He said, "You have me, sissy."

108

At the border Chloe swelled with excitement. She said, "We're about to be in Mexico. I can't wait to be in Cancun. Sand and sunshine could make me feel a little better."

Rebecca said, "I hope so, baby. You were crying in your sleep again. Do you remember your dreams?"

"It's always the same couple of things."

"What are they?"

"I see Peter's smile, then the blood. I see the kids covered in it. I see that paramedic curling up when I shot him." Chloe's eyes filled with tears. She asked, "Do you think I'm going to Hell?"

"No, baby, don't think things like that."

Chloe turned away and looked out the passenger side window. She spoke in a distant tone almost too quiet to hear. She said, "I can't help it. I feel lousy. I even abandoned my children, signed over my rights to them. What kind of person am I?"

"I think you have the potential to be a great person, baby. We all make lousy decisions and mistakes, and sometimes life just runs us over. Besides, you do plan on going back for the kids, don't you?"

A thick silence filled the cab. Chloe turned and looked in Rebecca's inquisitive hazel eyes. She felt the intensity of her friend's focus, and the weight of the question. Chloe said, "I'm going back for them. We're going to Cancun first." Chloe leaned forward and turned the volume dial up until the beat of the subwoofers in back flexed the air and vibrated everything.

Rebecca smiled as she pulled closer to the check point.

109

Three and a half days across Mexico and they were entering Cancun. Chloe marveled at the tourist-filled resort they were to stay at. After the valet took the truck, Chloe and Rebecca checked into their deluxe double bedroom with ocean view. Rebecca had called ahead and reserved the room for the week. The view of the beach from the sliding glass door took Chloe's breath away. It defined the lap of luxury.

Chloe said, "I can't believe we're here. We really drove all the way to Cancun."

"I can't believe we're here either, baby. My butt is so numb. I'm going to take a nap. I hope you don't mind."

"It's fine. You deserve it. I'm ordering room service."

"Beautiful. The therapy begins."

Chloe's eyes filled with tears. Rebecca asked, "What's wrong, baby? Did I say something wrong?"

Chloe shook her head and bit her lip. She said, "I just can't believe how lucky I am to have you at a time like this."

"Don't think about it too much, baby. I haven't had

anyone to care about since my father passed. I love you."

Chloe crossed the room and embraced her friend. She said, "I love you, too."

110

Mila's frustration with her grandmother made her furious. She wanted to make a phone call. It didn't matter what her grandmother thought of Rebecca and her mother. Refusing her the privilege of a phone call made her feel caged and abused. All that gave Mila hope was the sound of Rebecca's voice telling her everything was okay. Being neglected the security of those comforting words put Mila in a sour mood.

Grandma Samantha came into the room. She said, "Get ready for dinner children."

Mila screamed. "I'm not eating dinner! I'm not eating until you let me call my mommy."

"Young lady. You don't call your mommy. You call your mommy's friend. You're still being punished."

Mila cried. "It's been a week. It's not fair."

Samantha clucked and popped her false teeth. She said, "So you don't want to eat?"

"No."

"You can't have anything later if you don't eat now."

"Fine."

"Okay, Missy. You make your own bed."

Samantha left the room, closing the door behind herself. Barry sat on the bed next to Mila. He said, "I'm not eating if you don't, sissy."

"You can eat. I'm not making you do anything."

Barry rested his head on Mila's shoulder. He said, "We can sneak the phone tonight."

"How can we do that? She takes it to her room."

"I'll get it if you want me to. I'm good at sneaking."

Mila listened to her brother breathe. She reached over and squeezed his hand. The heaviness that weighed in her heart began to lift. She said, "Okay, boo-boo. Let's get ready for dinner."

111

When Mila and Barry sat at the dinner table, Samantha stared at Mila like the child had grown a third eye. Trying to ignore her grandmothers gawking, Mila didn't make eye contact. Grandpa Martin said, "Let's say grace."

Samantha said, "One second. Mila, why are you at my table?"

Mila began tearing up. She said, "I'm hungry."

"I don't think so, missy. After all that screaming and fit throwing. Go to your room, you don't get dinner tonight."

Mila stood and ran to her room crying. Barry threw his plate to the ground. The loud shatter of glass made Samantha jump in her seat. Barry said, "I hate you."

Grandpa Martin rushed around the table and snatched Barry up. He began swatting him hard. Barry cried out and Mila came running back into the dining room. She screamed, "Put him down! Leave my brother alone!"

Grandpa Martin dropped Barry and began pulling his belt off. He said, "Are you ready for yours?"

Mila had never been whipped. She ran to her room and slammed the door. Slinking to the floor shaking and frightened, she couldn't get the image of Barry getting spanked to leave. Grandpa Martin pushed the door open, and gave Mila her first beating. She screamed and cried, but he wouldn't let up.

When it was over, Barry was thrown in the room with her. The children huddled together, crying. Mila said, "W-we can't stay here. We have to l-leave tonight."

112

Late in the night, Mila and Barry lay awake listening to each other breathe. Mila whispered, "It's time, boo-boo."

The children climbed out of their bed and picked up the backpacks they had filled with clothes earlier. Mila put her finger to her lips, signaling Barry to be quiet. They opened their bedroom door. It squeaked louder than Mila remembered and made the hair on the back of her neck stand. She stood still for a moment to listen for her grandparents. The house was eerily silent.

Walking as slowly and quietly as they could manage, the children made it through the living room and to the front door. Mila turned the knob and the cuckoo clock on the living room wall began going off, signaling midnight. Startled, the children both jumped and lit out through the doorway, letting the screen door slam behind them.

Tearing a path through the flower patch and then across the yard, Mila turned to Barry. She said, "We've got to hide, boo-boo. Follow me."

They ran a couple of houses down. The house they

ran beside had shrubbery. Both children climbed and clawed their way into the bushes. They stayed as still and quiet as they could, breathing hard and trying to stay calm. Mila whispered, "We can't let them catch us now, boo-boo. They'll beat us for sure."

After a few moments passed they could see their grandfather Martin on the sidewalk with a flashlight. Mila prayed to herself that he wouldn't spot them. His beam passed over the bushes and he kept walking. Several moments later they saw a police car pass. Mila whispered, "We have to move. Maybe we should go in the back yard."

Barry said, "I'm ready."

The children began to get out of the bushes. The noise of the leaves made them pause. Mila said, "We're gonna get caught if we stay here."

Barry didn't say a word. He scrambled out of the shrubbery and through the gate of the back yard. Mila followed suit. In the yard the children were amazed at what they found. There was a large structure that stood two stories tall with a balcony. It looked like a child's large playhouse. They went inside through the front door and closed it behind themselves.

Mila said, "They won't find us here, boo-boo."

Barry asked, "How long do you think we can stay here?"

"I don't know. Maybe until mommy comes for us."

They looked around. A couch and small refrigerator with a bowl of fruit on top occupied the room. There were bananas, apples, oranges and pears in the fruit bowl. Water bottles and juice boxes filled the refrigerator. A small ladder led to the top of the structure. There were two plush cushioned chairs and book shelves occupying the top floor. Mila and Barry smiled at each other. They had found a utopia for their escape and refuge.

Mila said, "Tomorrow I'll try to get in the house and use the phone. Aunt Rebecca won't leave us like this. Neither will mommy when she finds out what happened. Don't worry, boo-boo."

"I'm not worried. If they don't get us, we can live here."

Mila giggled. She said, "Boo-boo, we'll be lucky if we can stay here for two or three days. It's a nice thought, though, this place is awesome."

"Well, I think we could stay here forever."

Mila rolled her eyes. "You would think that."

113

Chloe came in from the beach, drying her hair and wearing a one-piece swimsuit and a smile. Rebecca lounged in one of the comfortable hotel chairs, with one of her long legs draped across the arm in her light blue bikini, beaming at the sight of her happy friend over the rim of some non-fiction real estate book she'd been studying. Both women had been on the beach at sunrise. Chloe had stayed out, walking up shore a few miles and back, alone, as she requested.

Rebecca said, "It's good to see that pretty smile. How many times do you brush your teeth in a day?"

Chloe was caught off guard by the question. She asked, "Why? Does my breath stink?" She crinkled her nose.

Rebecca said, "No, baby, nothing like that. I was just wondering how you keep your teeth so white."

"I doubt they're whiter than yours, Becca. Yours are like neon lights or something. It's kind of intimidating. You look carnivorous when you smile."

"Good. I am carnivorous." Both women laughed.

Rebecca's phone started ringing. Chloe said, "I

thought you were going to turn that thing off."

"I don't want to be completely out of contact with the world, baby. What if it's the kids?"

Chloe rolled her eyes and threw her towel on the bed. She said, "Answer the damn thing then, I'm getting in the shower."

When Chloe emerged from the shower she felt refreshed. The ugly feeling of hopelessness that had been pulsing through her veins seemed to be slowly subsiding. Taking a deep breath, she wiped the condensation off the bathroom mirror and looked at herself. Being without Peter left a void in her heart, but she knew that eventually she would be able to heal, no matter what kind of ugly scar it left behind. She decided not to put on any makeup. Exiting the bathroom, she immediately read something amiss on Rebecca's expression.

Rebecca said, "Sit down, baby."

Chloe asked, "What's wrong?"

"Sit down, and I'll tell you."

Chloe took a seat at the edge of one of the beds. Rebecca said, "The kids are missing."

Startled and in disbelief, Chloe bit her lip. She asked, "Is that who called? The police? What do we do?"

"It was your in-laws who called. They wanted to know if the children were with us. I called and booked us a flight back. We'll be in town by this afternoon."

"What about the truck?"

"Fuck that truck, baby. I'll send for it, or come back. I don't care if we lose it, the kids are more important.

Don't you agree?"

"Of course."

"Beautiful. We're going to go get the kids. Get dressed and we'll go to the airport."

"Okay. I'm so sorry."

"Baby. You have nothing to be sorry about. I love your rug rats. I'm going to be pissed if anything happens to them. I might murder your in-laws in their sleep."

Chloe felt anxious hearing Rebecca's comment. Rebecca said, "Baby, it's a figure of speech. I'm not going to kill your in-laws."

"Promise?"

"Yes. I promise."

114

The club house mid-day grew hot enough to make the children sweat. They went up the ladder and opened the door to the balcony. A semi-cool breeze flowed in and refreshed them. Mila swigged a cold water from the fridge and Barry enjoyed a juice box. Mila studied the home that the club house belonged to, as well as the neighboring residences. She didn't see anyone moving around.

Mila said, "I'm going to try to get a phone, boo-boo. You stay put and I'll be back."

"I want to go."

"No. Stay here. I'll be back, quick."

"Okay."

Mila left the club house and went to the back door of the residence. She checked the knob and it was locked. Paranoia overtook her, she went back to the club house. She went up to where Barry had been watching her. Sitting next to him, she let out a defeated sigh.

She said, "I don't know what we're going to do."

He said, "Don't worry. We'll be okay."

Mila began to cry. She said, "If we can't talk to Aunt Rebecca, grandma and grandpa might get us."

Barry shook his head. He said, "I'm not going back there."

"They'll make us go back, boo-boo. We're just kids."

"If they do, I'll do something really bad."

Mila put her face in her hands. She said, "They might send us to foster care. Who knows how those people will treat us. We have to reach mommy."

115

Samantha and Martin Apple were livid. Martin said, "Can you believe these little shits? What kind of stunt do they think they're pulling? The next whoopin' they get is gonna be ten times worse, I can tell you that much."

Samantha said, "Maybe we should give 'em away. Let the state deal with 'em. I don't think the check is worth all this trouble."

"It's not just about a check, Samantha. You know that. These are Peter's kids."

"Martin, Peter hasn't talked to us in years. We barely met that little heathen Barry. I think we ought to cut our losses. If their own mother doesn't want them, why should we carry the burden? It's more about the money than anything. I say we give 'em up."

116

Chloe and Rebecca stepped off the plane at DFW International Airport and took a shuttle to Avis rental car. They picked up a coupe. Rebecca tested the car's limits getting to Martin and Samantha Apple's home. Outside the residence, Chloe steadied herself. She said, "I hate dealing with these people. I don't know what I was thinking leaving the children with them."

Rebecca said, "Don't beat yourself up about it, baby. We're here now. We'll get the kids back."

"There was the balance of Peter's life insurance funds. I promised it to Samantha and Martin if they kept the kids for six months. They're not going to sign the kids over now."

"Fuck the money, baby. If it's a money thing, we'll handle it. How much is it?"

"Thirty-thousand or so. I can't ask you to pay it."

"Baby, are you really worried about me spending money on you?"

"I'd pay you back if you did."

"Nonsense. You can have everything I have. We can share everything; you don't ever have to owe me anything."

"I don't know why you're so good to me."

"I already told you why I'm so good to you, baby. Do you want to hear it again?"

"Yes."

"I love you, baby."

Chloe smiled. She replied, "I love you, too, Becca."

"Beautiful. I want to propose something."

"What?"

"Can I adopt Mila and Barry?"

"You want to take the kids from me?"

"No, baby. Never. I just want to be a legal guardian, so nothing like this happens ever again. Is that okay?"

Chloe sat in deep thought for a moment. She asked, "Do you think you'll change your mind about us?"

"Never."

"Okay, let's do it."

"Beautiful. Now, shall we deal with the in-laws?"

117

When Rebecca and Chloe approached the door to Samantha and Martin's residence, the couple met them at the threshold. Samantha said, "I don't know what you two are doing here. The kids aren't here and there's nothing you can do."

Chloe said, "We'll find them, and when we do, I want my rights back."

Martin said, "You've signed over all your rights. You're a basket case, the courts won't be giving you custody over us. Why don't you take your little girlfriend and run along? We only called to make sure they didn't run to you."

Chloe said, "I know what this is about. If you want money, we've got it, we just want the kids."

Martin said, "Are you trying to tell me you have thirty grand you want to hand over?"

Rebecca said, "If you relinquish custody to me, I'll pay you fifty."

Chloe gasped. She said, "Becca, that's too much."

"Baby, it's nothing for those kids."

Martin said, "If you're serious, we'll give you

custody, but we never want to see any of you again."

Chloe covered her mouth. She said, "You're some of the worst people I've ever known."

Samantha said, "Missy, we never signed our kids over to anyone. We raised our own."

Chloe shook her head. She said, "Peter told me how you raised your kids. I don't know what I was thinking. You're both abusive sadistic assholes."

Martin said, "No matter what you think of us, those kids are ours until we've got cash in hand."

Rebecca shuddered. She said, "You'll get your cash, and you don't have to worry about hearing from any of us again."

Back in the car, Chloe shook with frustration. Rebecca said, "That was pleasant."

"I can't believe those people. This is blackmail."

"Baby, you knew what it would be. It's worth fifty-thousand to get rid of those two."

"Why did you offer so much? I don't like it."

"I made an offer they couldn't refuse. Now we have to find the children. We could go door to door or put up posters. What do you want to do?"

"I don't know what to do."

"Okay. Let's start in the neighborhood and talk to as many people as we can, first we'll go to the print store and make reward fliers."

"Okay, Becca. You're the brains, let's do it."

118

Mila woke and wiped sweat from her brow. She looked out the balcony door and saw there were people moving around inside the home the club house belonged to. To her horror, a young boy exited the home from the back door, his course directly to the structure they occupied. Mila went to the chair Barry slept in and shook him.

Barry woke startled. Mila put her finger over her mouth signaling for him to be quiet. The young boy could be heard in the lower level. He yelled, "Dad! Someone's been in my club house!"

Mila looked out the balcony again and could see the boy's father walking to the club house. Mila shook, terrified. The sound of the boy's father climbing the ladder to the upper level was like the sound of approaching doom to her ears. He spotted the children. He said, "What are you kids doing in here? Do you know you're trespassing?"

Mila pleaded, "Please, let me call my mommy. She'll pick us up."

The man said, "Come on down. I don't know what

kids think now days. You can't do anything you want."

"I know, we're really sorry. Can we please call?"

"Come on down. We'll get this sorted out."

Mila and Barry climbed down and the man looked at his son. He said, "Corbin, go get the cordless."

The boy ran in the house to get the phone. The man spoke to Mila and Barry, in a stern tone. He said, "You know, people get shot for trespassing. You're lucky I'm being nice. I could call the police."

Mila said, "I'm sorry. We're really scared. My mommy can talk to you. I'm not a bad girl."

"I believe you, kiddo. You can't go around breaking into people's property, though."

Corbin returned with the cordless phone and, with shaking hands, Mila dialed Rebecca's number.

119

Chloe and Rebecca stood in line at the print store with a flier to get duplicates made. Rebecca drew it up with a hefty reward to anyone who led them to retrieving the children. Chloe fidgeted, nervous anxiety drove her to pull her pills from her purse and crack open a bottled water. Rebecca stood calm and composed as ever.

Chloe asked, "How do you do it?"

"Do what, baby?"

"How do you stay so calm?"

Rebecca looked at her with that curious gleam in her eyes. She said, "One of us has to be the composed one. I don't mind filling the role."

Rebecca's phone began ringing. She looked at it and didn't recognize the number. She said, "Interesting. Let's see who this might be."

When she heard Mila's voice, relief washed over her. Rebecca said, "Tell me where you are, baby. Everything's going to be okay."

120

When Chloe and Rebecca pulled up to the house just half a block down from Samantha and Martin's home, Chloe breathed a sigh of relief. She asked, "Do you think they'll ever forgive me for leaving them?"

"You did what you thought you needed to. Forgive yourself, they'll forgive you."

"I hope you're right."

At the door a kind lady showed them inside. Mila bounded off the couch when she saw her mother and Rebecca. She ran to Chloe and began crying. She said, "Please, Mommy. Let us go with you. We'll be good."

Tears spilled down Chloe's cheeks. Barry walked to Rebecca and took her hand. He said, "I didn't think you would come back."

They left the residence after a short conversation with the couple. In the car, Chloe smiled at Rebecca. She asked, "What next, Becca?"

"Let's pay off the despicable in-laws and go to Cancun. What do you say?"

Mila asked, "Are we all going?"

Rebecca said, "I'm not letting you out of my sight,

baby."

Chloe leaned over and hugged Rebecca. She said, "I love you, Becca. Let's do whatever you want."

"Beautiful. We'll go to Cancun and then buy a house."

Mila asked, "Are we gonna live with you, Aunt Rebecca?"

Rebecca said, "Baby, we're all going to live together. Me, you, your mother and brother. What do you think about that?"

Mila said, "See, boo-boo. I told you they were coming for us."

"You were right, sissy."

Chloe said, "Let's go get some sand in our toes."

121

Elvin Craig stood in the holding cell with three other inmates. They were all waiting to hear from their lawyers. It was the first court appearance and he expected to hear some outrageous numbers. Maybe even the death penalty.

One of the men's lawyers came to the caged opening in the cell and offered the man twenty years. The man declined the deal. The lawyer shook his head and agreed to go back to the DA and ask for less time. Elvin hoped he would be offered twenty, even thirty years, he would take it in a heartbeat.

Elvin's lawyer came to the window. Walking over with an expectation of a life sentence, Elvin felt pressure inside his chest. The lawyer said, "Mr. Craig, the DA is offering you forty years. If it wasn't for your mental status it would be more."

Elvin asked, "Could we take it to trial?"

"Mr. Craig, if you go to trial, the DA says he will go for the death penalty. I'm going to be direct with you. If you don't take this, you will most likely end up with a life sentence or on death row. You will come up for parole within twenty years of the plea bargain with this deal. With good behavior, you could be home with plenty of years of life left to do whatever you want. It's up to you, though. We can turn down the deal."

Elvin looked at the floor and furrowed his brow. Thinking about his options and all the lawyer had said, he knew the deal was the best he would get. Looking the lawyer in the eyes, Elvin grimaced. He said, "Bring me the papers, I'll sign."

TO BE CONTINUED …

DON'T MISS THE NEXT INSTALLMENT IN THE UGLINESS TRILOGY!

Book Two: Choppy Waters

Scheduled for release in January, 2018

CHOPPY WATERS

PREVIEW

CHAPTER 1

Chloe's skin baked in the warm sun and she wished it could warm her frigid heart. Over a week in Cancun and the ache inside seemed to grow by the day. She missed Peter worse than she could have ever imagined missing anyone. Looking to her left and down the beach, she could see Rebecca playing in the sand with Barry. The sight of Barry frustrated her. Deep inside her dying heart she knew it wasn't really his fault. Peter's life had been taken by an unhinged lunatic. No one could have seen it coming. The haunting compulsion to blame Barry's behavior for everything that was happening to their now broken family turned her stomach.

Snapping out of her negative thoughts, she turned her gaze to the right and searched the sands for Mila. The sight of her daughter's frail figure coming down the beach gave her pause—she was scanning the beach for her mother. Chloe became alarmed as the girl began running full speed toward her, yelling, "Mommy, Mommy!" Standing quickly, Chloe ran to meet her. She grabbed Mila and searched her for wounds, then relaxed and let Mila catch her breath.

Chloe asked, "What's the matter, sweetie?"

Mila panted, and said, "I saw Aunt Gracie."

Chloe shook her head. She said, "That's impossible, sweetheart. Grace has been missing for years."

"I'm almost for sure it was her, Mommy. You have to come look before she leaves."

"Where is she?"

"She's way over there." Mila pointed to a couple sitting in beach chairs.

Chloe sighed. She said, "Okay. Let's go look. We're just going to walk by close enough to see, though. I don't want to be bothering anyone."

"Yes, let's go. I was so little the last time I saw her, but I know you'll know for sure."

Chloe took Mila's hand and glanced back over to Rebecca and Barry. Barry was busy burying Rebecca in sand. She shook her head and headed in the direction of the couple. The thought that Grace could be alive and well made Chloe's heart flutter. She felt a slight glimmer of hope.